LAST CHANCE

Once he had been Commodore Johnathan Braysen, commander in Earth's Space Force, legendary for his brilliant intellect and fighting skills.

Now he was simply John, a human derelict on the planet Drongail, gone sick and stale after years of ceaseless, senseless slaughter, a hopeless addict of the native drug called *dron,* his brain dulled, his nerves burned out, believing in no one and nothing, not even himself.

This was the only man who could lead the last men of Earth against the mightiest power in space—with the fate of the human race hanging on every move he made. . . .

RECALL NOT EARTH

C. C. MacAPP

A DELL BOOK

Published by
Dell Publishing Co., Inc.
750 Third Avenue, New York, N.Y. 10017

Dell ® TM 681510, Dell Publishing Co., Inc.
Printed in the United States of America
First printing—March 1970

(1)

He was a fairly tall man, hence considerably taller than the brown-skinned, hairless, wide-faced Dronthen passersby, who skirted wide of him half in scorn and half in prudence. He had the thinness of the derelict. The reddish-blond stubble on his rather prominent chin was at least ten days old. His shaky fingers were stained cinnamon-brown from *dron*. He kept swallowing and moistening his lips with his tongue, as if he suffered from the thirst-that-was-not-thirst, the chief symptom of *dron* need. Such symptoms were not surprising—he'd been on the planet Drongail for almost one of its years (slightly shorter than an Earth year), he'd become addicted almost at once, and he had not enjoyed the gentle forgetfulness of the almost narcotic *dron* for many days now.

He leaned against a wooden building, just inside the mouth of a littered alley, in the shade. This planet's sun was a little more than his skin could take. The building against which he leaned had no windows below the second story and no entrances except the one heavy-planked flush door. The alley behind him reeked of stale cooking grease, the body odors of more than one alien race, and (most of all) *dron*. That latter smell he held in vague affection—not only because, when he could get it, *dron* gave him some measure of comfort, but also because it reminded him of musty hay. That was one of the smells he remembered all the years since Earth.

A bit of paper blew against his bare ankle. He peered down at it (an empty *dron*-tube wrapper) and kicked it away irritably. When he looked up he saw a half-grown

Dronthen boy staring at him from ten paces away. "Observe well, urchin!" he snarled in the local dialect. "Ere you sport a pot belly, we'll all be extinct. And you shall not behold our like again!"

The stripling blinked and edged farther away.

The man turned and shuffled a few steps into the alley to sit down with his back against the building. For the hundredth time he fumbled in a pocket of his ragged coat, brought out a badly wrinkled slip of paper, smoothed it out, and peered at the writing. "John Braysen," it read, "it's urgent that I see you. I'll be at the north end of the alley you live in, two hours after noon tomorrow. B. Lange."

He thrust the note back in his pocket. "John Braysen," he muttered, as if his own name were strange. "Commodore Johnathan Braysen. Commanding Officer, Scout Wing, Terran Space Force." How long since he'd called himself anything but "John"? How long since he'd even been asked if he had a last name? Such records as were kept on Drongail (or on the last several alien worlds he'd drifted to) said merely, "John, native of Terra. Currently without citizenship. Vagrant. No listed crimes. No listed skills."

And how long since he'd seen Bart Lange? Four Terran years? No—they'd been together as mercenaries with the Hohdan Fleet, that time more than thirty of the surviving men had died, and that had been five years, give or take a few months, after the Destruction. Three years ago, then.

John murmured in vague bewilderment. Was the Destruction only eight years ago? That would leave him only thirty-seven—and he certainly felt older than that! It all seemed so long ago, so terribly long ago.

He wondered why Bart Lange wanted to see him. For the first few years after the Destruction, the only survivors—fewer than five hundred men of the Fleet—had stuck together. And then, when the necessities of survival in alien space split them apart, they'd looked forward eagerly to any reunion. Later, with the steady growth of despair and hopelessness, they'd mostly become apathetic about seeing one another. Vaguely, he wondered how many were still alive. The last he'd heard, a hundred or so had still been serving as mercenaries with various alien fleets; and the whereabouts of perhaps sixty or seventy more was definitely known. The rest—however many remained—were lost, scattered on backward worlds like Drongail.

He was surprised that Lange had been able to locate him at all—though, of course, cargo ships of many worlds stopped at Drongail, the source of *dron*. If Lange had any money—and he must, to make his way here—he'd be good for a touch. Vaguely John wondered whether he shouldn't spend the money on food, some simple garments (though an unexpected pang knifed through him at the thought of parting with this ancient coat of Earth origin); pay off some of the indigent's indebtedness at the grimy public flophouse where he lived. He could kick the *dron* habit, he thought, if he really made up his mind. But why bother? It wouldn't make any difference that mattered.

He stared idly at the line of shadow down the middle of the alley. Not time yet for Lange (if he showed up at all). John let his head droop forward, and dozed.

"John! John?"

John raised his head, blinking away sleep. It took his eyes a minute to focus on the stocky man in the neat blue suit. No—a zipperall garment, cut to the Fleet undress pattern! He struggled to his feet. Now that he was actually looking at Bart again, memories flooded back. Emotion welled up in him, tightened his throat, tried to burst out in sobs. He fought them down, blinked away tears, and seized the outthrust hand. "Bart! It's been so . . . It's wonderful to see you, Bart!"

Bart's face was serious and a little shocked. John felt himself flush. "Yes, I'm a *dron*-head, Bart. An indigent; a —a public charge. I get my meals, such as they are, and a pad to sleep on. Once in a while they take some of us out for a day or two of ditch-digging or levee-building. But—" He let go of Lange's hand and stood looking at the man. "You look great, Bart! I'm happy to see you that way. Are you still a mercenary? With whom? Have you—" He looked Bart over. "You don't seem to have suffered any serious wounds."

Lange continued to stare at him anxiously. Then he said, "I was with Hohd again for a two-thousand-hour hitch recently. I came through in one piece and got paid off, so I'm prosperous. They didn't want me seen on Hohd just then, so I drifted. Right now I'm with a—well, with a colony on a planet called Akiel. I'm gathering together all the men I can, John—there are over twenty of us now, traveling and tracing, trying to bring the Fleet back together. The . . . ruler of Akiel wants us. All of us."

John stared at the other. "You know most of us have given that up, Bart. Killing, and more killing—grabbing planets, raiding, hauling away loot from worlds we haven't the slightest grudge against to other worlds we don't care a damn about. I don't think you'll get many."

Lange said earnestly, "I think we will, John. This time there's a real reason!"

John sighed. "I'm surprised to hear you talk that way. The last time I saw you . . ." He shrugged. If Lange didn't feel the uselessness, the emptiness, there was no sense in arguing. "Akiel. I never heard of the place. What is there about it to, well, inspire a man? Is this some great cause you've latched on to?" He paused, remembering. "We looked for causes, didn't we? And we found a seller's market. Trained, disciplined, we were—so dauntless we became a legend almost overnight. Because we didn't give a whoop whether we lived or died, just so long as we could find, or think we'd found, something worth dying for. But it wore off, Bart. At least, it did for me. And I thought it had for you too."

Lange glanced up and down the alley and bent a little closer. "This colony I'm with now is Chelki, John."

John stared down at the shorter man. "Chelki? You mean it's in—in the Vulmot Empire?"

"No, John. These are *free* Chelki—a colony the Vuls don't even know exists! There's an Omniarch almost twenty-two hundred years old, a couple hundred years older than any of his descendants, who are the colony. He's a Vul slave who escaped with a few ambions and covered his tracks well!"

Things suddenly churned inside John. He hadn't known there was so much feeling left in him. Slowly he turned and stared half-seeingly at the Dronthens who passed the mouth of the alley, peering in wide-eyed to see *two* of the aliens called "men." Finally he sighed and turned back to Lange. "I don't think I'd even want to hit the Vuls, Bart. Oh, I'll hate them as long as I draw a breath—I doubt you could find one of us who won't—but, after all, it wasn't individual Vulmoti who did it. And (I can say this now) we more or less asked for it. We blundered into space we knew nothing about. And when we found something we should have run from, we tried to fight instead, took up the challenge as if we were the mightiest power in the galaxy. After already being stupid enough to reveal where our home world was! And . . . Well, I doubt that the Vul commander who hit the Solar System knew that it was our *only* system."

Lange's face was hard now. "We agreed about that once, John—but I know more now. This fugitive Chelki has had spy contacts with the Vulmot Empire for two thousand years, John—*two thousand years!* He knew, shortly after it happened, about our little skirmish and the quick kill of Earth. He's told me the reason, the actual Vul decision. Having seen how we fought against odds, they didn't want us developing to a powerful empire. And they decided we weren't suitable to be enslaved or perpetually subjugated. They knew they were killing us, John—and they spent a lot of time making sure there was no breeding stock left. High-up heads rolled because *we*, a tiny fraction of the Fleet, escaped. They laughed with relief when they found there hadn't been any women among us. They searched the Solar System and its vicinity *meticulously* to make sure there were no other survivors!"

John found he was trembling. He forced his fists to unclench. After a minute he sighed. "Even so—it's done. If I suddenly came face to face with a Vul here, I'd no doubt punch and scratch and bite like a demented wildcat. But to try to pull myself together and go out hunting Vuls to fight —no, Bart. Maybe I'm just an empty bag; but I don't have that much left in me. I don't really care whether the Chelki remain slaves or not. And anyway, it's ridiculous to think we could make even the slightest dent on the Vulmot Empire."

Lange's face twisted with emotion. He stepped forward and seized handfuls of John's coat. "Listen to me, damn it —I'm not talking about some righteous crusade! *There are women alive!* More than a hundred of them, and practically all of child-bearing age! This Omniarch on Akiel knows where they are! He's willing to help us reach them!"

For just a moment blood pounded in John's temples. Then it subsided, and he laughed bitterly. "That old nonsense, Bart? You've fallen for that *again?* You must be cracking up. Don't you remember all the crazy rumors, the wild-goose chases we went on like a horde of rutting tomcats? What have you been— Look, the only thing *I'm* hooked on is *dron.* It befuddles your wits a little, and eventually eats away at your guts, but it doesn't make a child of you!"

Lange stepped back with a hard grin. "Listen to me, Commodore Johnathan Braysen, whose name was a byword, a few years ago, in alien military organizations all over this sector of the galaxy. You who outwitted all the brains of the Vul Task Force and tied them up in knots, using just a handful of small ships. You who could have had whole fleets at your disposal just by nodding and signing your name. The Chelki I'm dealing with knows all about you and says you're the man we need; you out of the bunch. He says *you* are the one who can rally us together." Lange paused for breath. "He was scheming for two millennia, long before Earth sprouted wings, let alone null drives—long before Columbus sailed three wooden ships across an ocean that hasn't so much as a living minnow in it now. We came as a windfall to him. *He* engineered the rescue of these women. *He* caused a force of slave Chelki to land on Earth with forged authorization and take a few thousand females, mostly young, for biological experimentation. *He* arranged for some of them to be spirited away, and the records changed to hide the discrepancy. Look, John—a lot of Chelki died protecting that deception. He's described the whole thing in detail to me, and shown me pictures!"

John felt a chill. Lange looked so sincere; yet . . . "Bart, be sensible. Does it stand to reason that this Chelki plotter, even if he *is* what he claims, would go to those lengths just to help an unimportant race survive? What are we to him?"

Lange snarled an obscenity. "Can't you see, John, we impressed the Vuls so much that they went to real pains to exterminate us. You don't exterminate anything that's not a threat. The Omniarch sees us as a long-range threat to the Vuls. We're not the *whole* of his plan—I don't doubt he's got a hundred other little things going. But he wants us to survive! We've already demonstrated that we stack up very well, as warriors, against other species. Look at it from the Omniarch's viewpoint!"

John, the blood beginning to pound in his temples again, stared at Lange. Could all this actually be true—a fact, not just another desperate dream?

It sounded so improbable. Still, the *chance*—the bare, infinitesimal, incredible, long-abandoned blessed chance . . .

Suddenly John was weeping.

(2)

THE SMALL SHIP (a patched-up old Unarmed Scout re-
tired from the Hohdan Fleet and given to Bart Lange as
part payment for his services) broke out of null about a
tenth of a light-year from Akiel's sun, took bearings, made
a short zeroing-in hop, and broke out again practically in
orbit around the planet. It was a blue-green world—vastly
jungled in places, grassy in others, with no really large
seas but with many small ones and a myriad of lakes and
rivers. There were minor ice caps at both poles. Only a
few small brown areas near the equator interrupted the
verdure. The atmosphere was rather thick, considering
the surface gravity of slightly less than one gee, and the
hothouse effect obviously made for temperate climates.
There were no impressive mountain ranges.

No spaceport facilities were visible even from as low as
five thousand feet.

Bart Lange punched out a landing program on the
simple computer keyboard, scanned the playback on the
data screen, and turned to John. "If any unwanted visitors
showed up here, they'd actually have to land to find any
signs of technology. No radio, no visiocasts, no exposed
factories or dwellings. Not even any centralized power
sources to spill detectable energy into space. Anyway, this
star's not near any well-traveled routes. The Omniarch tells
me that in all the time he's been here only four exploration
ships have broken out within mass-detector range, and
only one of them came close enough in to take pictures."

John—considerably neater now, and less shaky of hand,
though there were still moments when he felt the *dron*

need—ran his eyes over the small ship's instruments. "If they keep mass detectors in orbit around their sun, they must really be masters of miniaturization. That one blip in the corner of screen H-four could be a chunk of rock the size of your fist. How do their detectors report, anyway? Do they have a lock-on to the planet so they can beam transmissions in?"

Bart nodded. "Right. To intercept a beam you'd have to pass directly in line at the moment of squirting." He reached up to turn knobs manually, zooming in a view of a grass plot below. "Can you spot the landing field?"

"No."

Bart grinned. "As soon as we're in and under cover, they'll resod what marks we leave. If there are any precautions they don't take, I can't think of them!"

The ship slowed, hovered, then settled slowly to within inches of the ground. Views on screens began to move sideward. Then the hazed, rather yellowish sunlight was blocked off. An overhead viewscreen showed a shifting image of large spade-shaped leaves.

And then they were over a concrete ramp and slanting underground. Daylight, behind them, was cut off as doors closed, and artificial light took over. The ship moved a little way and settled to a concrete floor.

Bart jabbed keyboard studs, and air began to hiss in. There was a mild pungency, possibly from traces of ozone, and a leafy smell. The hissing faded quickly.

Bart eyed John for a moment, as if to make sure he was over the *dron* shakes, then opened hatches. John, peering out, got glimpses of vague dark-furred forms—then a big Full Male Chelki paced into sight.

John peered at the being. This was a patriarch, all right! He must weigh eight hundred pounds. The skin on the face was like gray leather, and four legs each as thick as a man's thigh.

John remembered the first time he'd seen a Chelki. It had been a shock. They had legs not too different from those, say, of a hairy bovine, and a barrel-shaped body, but there any similarity ended.

The neck and head weren't in the right place at all—
they grew out of a mound atop the *middle* of the body.
From this mound also grew two arms, good-sized ones,
ending in large, hairy, deft hands with three fingers and a
thumb each. The feet weren't hoofed; they had toes like an
ostrich's. There was no tail, and no chest at the front end
of the body; in fact, you could distinguish the front end
only by the way the feet aimed and the head faced (though
the rather long neck could twist enough to let a Chelki
face completely to his rear). The organs of elimination
and reproduction were below the body, though you
couldn't see that at a glance. The face was perhaps not
humanoid, but it wasn't too far from it.

The thin-lipped mouth opened and produced precise,
faintly accented English. "Welcome to Akiel, Commodore
Johnathan Braysen. I have waited long for this day." The
voice was deep, slow, mellow. "Let us go to a place where
you can sit down."

As they crossed the concrete floor of the underground
hangar, they passed a number of Chelki of much smaller,
lighter build—neuter-gendered workers who showed no
curiosity about John. There were also individuals of similar body form but obviously more active minds; their
heads were actually bigger, and they looked at John
closely, inclined their heads in a sort of greeting, blinked
slowly at the Omniarch (a sign of deference, John knew)
and in some cases carried tools or instruments that
marked them as technicians, not simple workers. Then
there were a few individuals almost as big as the Omniarch
himself, but with claws on toes and fingers, and short
snouts on their heads equipped with combative-looking
teeth. These were the Warriors—male gender, though
they did not breed—and they carried pistols in belts or
cinches that circled their round bodies. There was one
other Full Male besides the Omniarch, younger and
smaller than the latter, but no females in sight.

John knew that the Chelki had some of the propensities
of social insects, such as bees or ants—but much more! A
Full Male not only fathered a large number of offspring

but also could produce in his own body hormones to make those offspring any of various sexes and genders. The newly born Chelki was called an "ambion," and could be caused by the Full Male to develop into any of the various types. There were other complexities which John didn't understand.

But the highest intellect was in the Full Male.

John and Bart sat in chairs quite suited to humanoids (of which there were many species in this sector of the galaxy). There was a small table holding a carafe of lightly fermented juice and three glasses.

The Omniarch, of course, stood. He looked at John for a few moments in a serene way, smiling the Chelki smile (which was tight-lipped, not showing the herbivore teeth). "I do not believe you have suffered much from your liaison with *dron*. I was worried about that."

John's face grew warm. "I feel all right. Bart Lange here tells me you have photographs to show me."

"I have." The big Chelki paced to the table, pushed the carafe to one side, and laid down the folder he was carrying. "There is a series, showing the taking of the females —you will note their ages, a few being hardly more than infants—the experimental facilities, and some of the corpses. I regret that there is considerable unpleasantness. I assure you we Chelki would not have participated had there been any other way." He shuffled photographs—convincing ones, in color.

John went rigid, then began to tremble with anger. Some of the things . . . He glared up at the Omniarch. "You planned this—this slaughter?"

"I cannot deny that I foresaw it, John Braysen, though Vulmotean medical experimenters ordered it. Please look at the rest of the pictures. Here are several showing the group of females we spirited away from the experimental stations." Those did indeed show girls and women—and a few infants—being escorted by Chelki of Technician and Warrior genders. And one last picture showed, presumably, the place to where they'd been taken—an ordinary-looking meadow with some unordinary bushes in the background.

John, still trembling, pushed the photographs from him. "All right—tentatively I'm convinced! But Bart tells me that you won't take us to the women yet, nor tell us where they are. In other words, we have to do things for you first!"

The Chelki blinked twice—the sign of affirmation. "I ask you to understand that my plans are long and complex and difficult and leave me very little room for being considerate. I hope you will not balk at what part you are asked to play."

John swallowed to relieve the thirsty sensation that neither fermented juice nor water could cure. "At least you're frank. But why won't you tell us what circumstances the women are in?"

One of the big hairy hands rubbed idly at the base of the neck. "Because, John Braysen, there is danger that you may fall into Vulmotean hands. It would be tragic if they learned enough to decide to kill you on the spot. But it would also be tragic so far as my own species is concerned. And I hope you will agree to this: a few of you viable male specimens must stay on Akiel at all times. Believe me—the women are as safe as I could possibly arrange."

John sighed in exasperation. "All right, we're in no position to bargain. What is it you want us to do first of all?"

"First of all, I have arranged for you a bit of service for an old comrade of yours—Vez Do Han, Field Commander of Hohdan Strategic Defense Forces. There are some hit-and-run raids he finds expedient to assign to mercenaries. I have agreed to turn over to you a small number of ships I have acquired over the centuries: eight Vulmotean Armed Scouts, and one *Nave*-class vessel of sixty thousand Terran tons. That capital ship is old but has been updated with new rupter beamers and laser clusters. She's partly stocked with missiles, and Hohd will supply more. And Vez Do Han will be happy to let you keep any vessels you can capture."

John sighed. "You say *you* arranged this with Vez Do Han?"

"Yes. I have been quite useful to him, and to his predecessors, in the field of espionage. He does not know the location of Akiel, and I ask that you not inform him. That will be desirable for you also, since a few men are to stay here, and you will want them to be as safe as possible."

John knew he was scowling. He looked at Bart, who said nothing. John looked at the Omniarch. "And what else will you want of us, when the job for Hohd is finished?"

"I shall," the big Chelki told him, "want you to help with a certain job of escorting unarmed ships. But that is not due yet. There will be, perhaps, minor bits of fighting before then."

"Minor fighting! It'll have to be, with only one capital ship and a few Armed Scouts!"

"Plus what you can capture—though I admit that may not amount to much. But I have more to offer."

"Well?"

The Omniarch returned the photograph to the envelope he'd taken them from, put the envelope in his folder, and laid the folder on the small table. "You have perhaps seen a few Klee artifacts, and heard various legends."

John shrugged. "Who hasn't? Bits of statuary, cast from metals no one can duplicate and that have lasted twenty or thirty thousand years without corroding. Smashed instruments that baffle the best of scientists. Kitchen implements, jewelry . . ."

"I," the Omniarch said, "know where I can get you a Klee ship, intact, powered, and operative. Not primarily a warship, though she has bays for weapons to be mounted. A very large ship. And I will help you solve the controls and instruments. I have made a considerable study of Klee technology and have made a few inroads."

John was suddenly sitting straight in his chair. "Are you serious? A Klee *ship?*"

"I am very serious. It is part of my plan."

John glanced at Bart, who looked astounded; glanced at the carafe on the table; decided that fermented juice wouldn't help the maddening thirst he felt. "When would you give us this ship?"

"When you have made the bargain with Vez Do Han. The ship may be very useful in the raids, though of course you will want to avoid its being seen—it would create the utmost in sensations, and set the whole sector to looking for you. Now, there is one little deception I suggest—other than that you *not* tell Vez Do Han about this ship. She must be obtained from a planet in the Hohdan region, and I need an excuse for going there. So do you. I suggest you ask from Vez Do Han, as part of the bargain, some uninhabited planet in the region. Not the one where we will get the Klee ship—some other, more suited to your species. You may even want to settle there while you replenish your species, after you are joined by the women."

John scowled at the big nonhumanoid. "I don't like the idea of deceiving Vez! He was always scrupulously fair with me."

"And with me; and I with him, until now. It is a necessity I can not see a way around. Ponder it, and I believe you will agree." The Omniarch, perhaps noticing John's repeated swallowing, came forward and refilled the glasses. "Now to another point: you may make this planet your base of operations until you are organized, then I ask that you go elsewhere—possibly to the planet Vez Do Han gives you. You can understand that I want as little traffic in and out of Akiel as possible."

John said uncomfortably, "All right. Will you be keeping in touch with us?"

"I will, though I must leave Akiel, for caution's sake, and go into hiding elsewhere now. But I will arrange an indirect, discreet chain of communications."

(3)

"Bunstill!"

"Here."

"Cameron!"

"Here, sir."

"Damiano!"

"Here."

THE MUSTER LIST blurred before John's eyes for a moment. There were so many missing names that came flooding back in his memory. Of course this wasn't a complete gathering of surviving men; there'd be others trickling in. But even including those, it would be such a thin roll call. . . .

He finished up with "Zeitner" (at least they had a "Z") and turned to look yet again at the looming hull of the sixty-thousand-ton *Nave*-class ship. She was a squat cylinder, as were most spaceships (for several practical reasons), with a height about the same as her diameter; which, not counting the various protuberances that were weapons bays and sensors, came to a little over two hundred feet. Not the biggest ship he'd ever seen, but far bigger than any that Earth had built in that brief spasm of arming when Earth thought she could fight back.

And, the Vulmoti being what they were, this ship wouldn't lack in any essential. There were no signs of exterior damage. No doubt she'd been seized furtively by Chelki, and her loss falsely accounted for.

He turned back to the men. "This will be our flagship, at least for the time being. *Luna,* we'll call her, because that was the first place our grandfathers went from Earth. But it wasn't the last!"

There was brief cheering.

"I've already told you that we have to reach those women by a long, roundabout path. What I haven't told you is that the first leg of the trip will be another job with Hohd. This time, though, we won't be interlarded with Hohdans or other aliens. We'll be raiders, on our own."

They stood waiting for him to continue. He saw various things on different faces—hope, skepticism, apathy, grim determination. There was no inspired excitement and no sullenness. *God,* he thought, *what a dried-out bunch we are.* Yet he knew that in each of them, as in him, the excitement lay buried, beneath the long years of despair.

He thought of many things he might say. He simply said, though, "Well, that's all for now. There'll be details on the bulletin boards."

The Chelki, under the direction of a Full Male who was second in command here on Akiel, had done an excellent job of refitting and conditioning the old Vul ship (and the eight smaller ones as well). The grav drive was tuned so precisely that John could lift the sixty-thousand-ton vessel a half-inch from the concrete floor of the vast grotto where she lay hidden and set her down again in increments of a quarter-inch, all without the slightest jar or sensation of inertia. Such tuning was important; in combat, a ship's computers (to say nothing of her flesh-and-blood pilots) might demand that she halt instantly, from a velocity of an appreciable fraction of light-speed, or dart away just as instantly on a different course. The gravs had to act upon every component (including passengers) at the same exact moment and with the same force, else she'd be torn apart or her passengers squashed by acceleration.

It was peculiar, he mused, how so many species (of humanoids, at least) discovered the grav drive (and related null drive) at about the same point in their technological development, almost as if it were programmed into the course of science.

"Drive Theory" was one of the courses he, like every cadet of his time, had taken at the academy. He felt he'd gotten as much out of it as most nonphysicists.

Mankind had developed the grav drive within a reasonable time after two monumental discoveries: first, that gravity was a *push*, not a pull; second, that the push could be screened off by a sheet of any of several special alloys under the influence of certain force fields distantly related to electricity.

This is why a push had always been mistaken for a pull: one of the basic facts of the "normal" universe is that all of space—every cubic centimeter of it, from all directions and all distances up to (and perhaps including) whatever "infinity" exists—repels matter. It repels matter ceaselessly, as if trying to squeeze it out of existence.

But, as if there were some conscious community of mutual assistance, each particle of matter shields every other particle against this push by space. That is as if one opaque ball cast a shadow upon another. And, while space shoves against matter from all directions, there is nothing correlated in this shove; no transverse action or other baffling peculiarity, as with the front of a light wave. Each discrete quantum of space aims a determined straight-line punch continuously at every particle, as if no other quantum of space existed. The punches do not get tangled up or canceled out or deflected. They do reinforce each other, but only in an additive straight-line way.

In one thing the old physics was partly correct: the force of a push does vary inversely with distance, but not in direct ratio or in the ratio of squares or cubes. The ratio, which can be measured with some accuracy by an ingenious experiment (which, incidentally, led to the invention of the mass detector), has something to do with the number of dimensions that exist in "normal" space. And that is not a matter to discuss casually.

So, the situation exists that every particle of matter is being shoved at from every direction, but is shielded to some tiny extent by every other particle. But the mutual shielding of two particles is only along the straight line joining them. Therefore, what can two particles do but move toward each other? Along that one line, the pressure upon them is lessened by a very small fraction.

Naturally, two electrons, for instance, separated by a distance of several thousand light-years, would take a very long time to come together (not even considering that they were not the only two particles in space). But time is long, and space is patient. Hence particles become atoms, and atoms molecules, and molecules solid masses (if one can stomach that latter inexactitude).

There are counterforces that prevent space from squeezing all matter into one inconceivable ball. One such force is inertia ("centrifugal force" in the case of two particles or rocks or stars orbiting each other). A second such force is the natural repulsion between particles having like charges: electron repelling electron; positron, positron. Another is the pressure of radiant energy, as in the terrific effort of a hot star to explode. And there are others not describable in such simple terms.

So, when a considerable mass has been pushed together, it has a considerable effect of shielding against space. For instance, a man standing upon a planet is partly shielded from almost one hundred and eighty degrees of space. The other half of space pushes him against the planet. Semi-primitive man, with his reasonable but unreliable tendency to see things as they appear, called this effect "gravity" and thought it was a pull by the planet. Null-age man, with his perhaps not reasonable propensity for the complex (fore-shadowed, maybe, by such utterly improbable developments as the internal-combustion engine), seized upon the true nature of "gravity" and put it to work (as had, long before, various other equally antipractical, venturesome, stubborn species).

All particles of matter act as natural shields against the push of space, but with limited efficiency. Artificial shields can be made that perform, at optimum, with awesome efficiency. Thus, if a person standing on Earth held a shield above his head and activated it, he would be propelled violently into the air by the residual "space push" penetrating the planet and shoving at him from below. So would a cone of soil (though, since the shielding falls off with distance from the shield, and also because of the geometry of the situation, the cone would not be very long).

The residual push penetrating Earth could be, and was, calculated at approximately two hundred and fifteen gees, and from that (assuming various things) it was clear that Earth, in effect, screened off slightly less than one-half of one percent of the push from half of space. Or: maximum theoretical "gravity," anywhere, was two hundred and sixteen gees.

John had never found that theory particularly reassuring. Two hundred gees, or considerably less, could make puree of a man!

(Note: it is possible to build a shield that will stop the push from one direction only. That is desirable in self-propelled missiles, in certain instruments, and in special tools.)

(Further note: due to certain peculiar properties of space and of shields, it is possible to design the latter to produce a "lee" of a particular shape: conical, spreading, parallel beam, and so forth. For instance, the use of high shielding and a long tapering cone, combined with the one-way effect, gives the weapon called the "rupter"—intense "push" is applied to the target or a small zone of it, and when the push is applied and interrupted and reapplied at a suitable rate, the target can be shaken to pieces. Rupters have ranges limited, in practice, to a few miles. Another example of special shields is in arranging "artificial gravity" within a ship. Without artificial gravity, passengers would suffer various discomforts, some fatal.)

Obviously, if you build a shield into or onto a structurally strong container, and activate it, the whole container will be urged, to some degree, in the direction of the shield. If you take a cylindrical tank of, say, one thousand gallons capacity, put an airtight hatch in it, and fit a shield flat upon one end, you have the fundamentals of a space-

ship. Such a ship, if the shield is designed for variable and
closely controlled input of power, can rise slowly and
gently from a planet's surface without pulling a divot of
the planet with it.

Commonly, ships are cylinders of high-strength steel,
less than twice as long as their diameters, with shields at
either end (occupying the full cross section as nearly as
possible) and smaller auxiliary plates at various points of
the cylindrical walls (and sometimes others distributed
along cross sections between the two ends). Application of
power to any shield or combination of shields is controlled
by a special computer, which is usually in turn controlled
by the main computer, since manual control might be
jerky and dangerous. A ship in space can achieve startling
acceleration, because passengers are accelerated by the
"space push" along with the rest of the ship. Anomalies
exist, off the axis of the ship, and at the rear; but these are
canceled or counteracted by properly designed and adjusted auxiliary plates. A combat ship can dart to the sides,
too, though not with the acceleration it can achieve along
its axis. Due to various limitations of structural materials,
power feed, passenger reaction, etc., acceleration (in
practice) is limited to about seventeen gees (in normal
space, that is). Seventeen gees is not enough to dodge a
swarm of computer-coordinated missiles, but it can make
them work.

The null drive is something else again. Very soon after
development of the new grav-drive technology and science,
there were several breakthroughs in understanding the
nature of space itself.

The real savants claimed that there must be quite a
number of "spaces," each positioned to the others in such a
way that time was involved, along with various dimensions.
John Braysen was willing to accept that without being
harangued at length about it.

There appeared to be no immediate prospect of switch-
ing from "normal" space (that is, "our" continuum) to
any of the other spaces. However, there was some kind of

limbo, or state of existence that was none of the spaces, into which an object could be shifted. The way this was done was awesome: the object (a ship and passengers, for instance) had to have every particle charged with a kind of energy related to, but not identical with, the field that produced gravity shielding. When this charge reached a critical intensity, a little extra surge caused it (to all exterior observations) to cease to exist in normal space. Passengers felt only an instant of odd disorientation.

In this strange limbo (called "null"), ordinary grav drives could accelerate the "ghost" of the ship at a rate fantastically greater than in normal space. That hull acceleration didn't require exceptional power, but to attain readiness for null *did*. Conduits to feed that power without melting had a practical limitation: the best rate of charging that Earth's or any other known technology could achieve was a little over four minutes.

So you couldn't "break out" of null and reenter immediately.

One of the puzzling things was that the tremendous power thus fed into matter could be discharged so instantly with very little detectable "spill." A little static, a momentary mild blue glow, were the only phenomena yet detected.

Travel in null was not instantaneous. There was a limit of some sort; and, to simplify as much as possible the terrible problems of navigation, the apparatus was standardized to fit some little-understood natural velocity that approximated four hundred and ninety light-years per hour. Usually a ship going, say, one hundred light-years, could judge its breakout point to within one-tenth light-year of its target. From there you made an additional short null hop or hops, like a golfer sinking a putt.

(4)

THE HOHDANS were humanoid, and in his past dealings with them it had seemed to John that they represented more or less what mankind might have become, given time to expand into space and acquire sophistication. Sophistication, not in the sense that the loose galactic-sector community of races with the null drive displayed uniformity of attitudes (far from it!), but sophistication in the sense of a certain rather cynical acceptance of war, intrigue, empire, and misadventure.

Vez Do Han was, physically, a typical Hohdan. He was three or four inches under John's six-feet-one, broad of shoulder though not thick through the chest from front to back, with a peculiar longness and unbunchiness of muscle that, to a human, disguised his real strength. His fingers (four to a hand plus a thumb, in a human-enough placement) did not taper as a man's did, but had instead somewhat flattened, spatulate tips and very strong and strongly rooted nails. Why that particular oddity had evolved, John could not guess.

The Hohd had hair on the greater part of their faces and bodies, but it was strange hair—short and branched, almost like downy feathers. It came in a range of colors. Vez Do Han's was medium gray with a bluish tinge. He, like other Hohdans, showed no tendency toward baldness.

Hohdan faces, like the faces of most humanoids, were a little disturbing to a man until he was used to them. The nose was triangular in profile, jutting forward from the face like some vane put there for steering. It was big enough, and thin enough, to reinforce that fancy. The nostrils (slits set close together on the lower slant) could close immediately as if to shut out dust storms. The chins were broad and square, the ears more elongated than a man's, the eyes smaller and more deeply recessed.

But Vez Do Han's grin was recognizable as such. So were his scowl and the piercing, scrutinizing look that he directed upon John.

"Aside from professional interest, Commodore"—this in casual Home Hohdan, an expressive though not delicate dialect that John spoke well enough—"it is a personal joy for me to see you again, and you looking so fit. I sought you once, a trifle over a year ago, and heard that you had become an addict on Drongail. I placed a mourning sheaf of black dragonweed on the bulletin board of my flagship for a ten-day."

John shrugged. "Yes, I was addicted. I didn't expect ever to come into space again. But I'm over it now." He wished that were strictly true.

Vez made the fist-opening gesture that meant affirmation or approval, meanwhile turning his small dark eyes toward the mass-indicator sphere of the dispatch ship they were aboard. "I see that two more of your flotilla have made breakout."

"Yes. I left word for them to null here—they were late for the previous rendezvous, as they were out rounding up a few more men—but I told them to show themselves first at a nonthreatening distance, so you'd not mistake them for spies or raiders. They're standard Vul Armed Scouts, with some new launchers for missiles installed. I suspect that the Chelki Omniarch, who arranged this meeting, gave you details."

"Yes, friend John Braysen. Frankly, I would prefer more laser clusters and fewer missiles—the whole point of these raids I contemplate is to throw suspicion upon the Vulmoti, and they are notoriously free with energy beamers—but that is not important. You possess details of our difficulty?"

John made the fist-closed negative sign. "He told me very little, in case I should fall into the wrong hands."

Vez grinned wolfishly. "Were I in his place—dealing not with you, old comrade-in-arms, but with someone I was meeting for the first time—I should have relied upon even firmer precautions, such as installing self-destruct mechanisms in the ships I gave you. But the Chelki are squeamish, which accounts in part, no doubt, for their enslavement. . . . Well, the Bizh Empire is centered about seven hundred light-years out along this spiral arm. That puts them almost directly across a thousand light-years, more or less, of Sparse Region, from the Vulmoti." He glanced again at the mass-detection sphere—a professional like Vez wanted always to know what was around him. "The Bizh are nonhumanoid, ten-limbed radial creatures with certain living habits that would be disgusting were they less fascinating. However, that is not our concern with them, nor do they pose any threat to Hohdan territory within the foreseeable future. They *are* impinging upon territory of two of our lesser allies, both humanoid. Not that body form would be a matter of blind prejudice with you, I know. . . . These allies have appealed to us for support; and, being that they occupy positions as buffers between us and the Bizh—and also, to some extent, the Vulmoti—"

John studied the alien face. "It seems a bit coincidental that the job we can do for you involves the Vulmoti."

Vez grinned. "Not at all. Surely you see the furry hand of the Omniarch in that? In his fixity of purpose, he has often stooped to interempire intrigue. It is *his* idea to implicate the Vulmoti, and it is a good one. It will keep the Bizh worried for a while."

John stared at his own hands. He felt as if they were shackled, with the Omniarch holding the keys. . . . He daren't tell Vez the whole of his own bargain with the Chelki. "All right. I'll study whatever particulars you've brought for me. Now . . . there's the matter of terms. We want to keep whatever ships and materials we can capture intact."

"Of course, friend John Braysen."

"And there's another thing. Our life spans are getting on, and we were scattered—and, as you learned, some of us were disintegrating fast. Our species will soon be gone. While we few last, it seems to me that we ought to draw together, help each other to keep what dignity we can, try to leave some monument, so to speak, other than scattered nameless graves. There may still be some literature in us, some song. . . . Some worthwhile benevolence, perhaps. We want a world somewhere, for our old age. And naturally we'd want it to be in some region that was at least tolerant of us."

Vez peered at him for a minute, then smiled. "I will accept that, tentatively, though it is a bit squashy for hard warriors like yourselves. Certainly we can pick out an uninhabited planet, suitable for you, somewhere within our region. That is all?"

"That is all," John lied unhappily.

"Good, then! I shall be seeing you again before you make the first raids. Oh! You need missiles, of course, and some fuel wire. And we ourselves have four Vulmotean ships to contribute—Armed Scouts, damaged in capture, sold to us by erstwhile skirmishers with the Vulmoti, and rebuilt. Until next joining, then?"

"Until next joining."

(5)

JOHN SCANNED through a set of figures on a single sheet of paper, glanced up at Bart's dissatisfied face, and looked at the figures again. "It's as good as we expected, Bart. Of two hundred and seventy-three we hoped to find, you've brought in two hundred and fifteen. Only nineteen of the list definitely dead, if those two sick cases pull through. Comparing the roster of the last encampment, deducting reported deaths, and applying percentages from these figures here, we can hope to find another forty or so alive somewhere."

Bart said, "I'd put it at another sixty-odd. I didn't want to talk about this until I saw you alone, because I'm not sure what effect it might have on morale, but on this last trip I got a lead on a couple dozen more, all on one planet."

John straightened in his chair and looked more closely at his second in command. "What's bothering you, Bart?"

"Well, I think we ought to make a decision about this group I heard about. They're on Jessa with Humbert Daal."

John suddenly felt thirsty. He spread his hands out flat on the desk and looked at them. They seemed steady. He said slowly, "I was thinking we'd just leave Humbert, and anyone who'd joined him, alone. He made himself very plain the second time we had a rumor about live women. I don't think we'd want him among us anyway, spreading his raven croaks."

"I agree, John. But the others with him don't necessarily all feel the same way. Some of them—Fred Coulter, I hear, and Ralph Sears—were with us the last time you and I fought together for Hohd."

"Oh. Well, did you try to send messages to them?"

"No. Being that Jessa's out in the other spiral arm, I thought I'd better talk to you first."

John nodded slowly. "It's a long way from the Vuls, but they do scout in that far now and then. Well, do you think you ought to make a trip out there and talk to them?"

"I wasn't thinking exactly that. I do think Coulter and Sears and any others who weren't definitely stooges of Humbert ought to be given the choice. But we ought to wait as long as possible; then maybe we should go there as a group. It would impress them more, I think." He hesitated. "John, do you think Humbert was actually a fag?"

John glanced at him quickly. "Oh, no. Definitely not! At least, he wasn't when he and I were at the academy together."

Bart said, "A lot of the men thought he was. After all, a poet . . ."

John swallowed and wished he had a slug or two of hard liquor. "Well, it wasn't so. His verse wasn't effeminate; and those of us who knew him when he was young never thought there was anything unmasculine about his writing poetry." John paused. The disagreement with Humbert was too clear in his memory for comfort. Besides, a part of him leaned toward agreement with the position Humbert had taken. "You know, Bart, if we don't make it—this thing involving the women, I mean, and Homo sapiens ends right here—it may be Humbert Daal's name that lives awhile among humanoid races. Nothing we've ever done except fight—none of the literature we brought with us, though God knows it was little enough—has caught on like his *Epitaph*." He was silent for a moment. "And mercenary warriors are a dime a dozen."

Bart said impatiently, "Sure. I'm just wondering how he'd react if we go out there and try to enlist some of his companions."

John took his hands off the desk and put them out of sight. "I definitely don't think we should take the whole fleet out there. A couple of small ships, maybe. We can leave the rest somewhere in the Sparse Regions, and rendezvous afterward. Too many alien cargo ships land on Jessa to load that fiber they grow."

Bart said, "I guess you're right." He stood up. "If you don't need me for anything right now, I'd like to get a little sleep."

"Of course."

After Lange had gone, John sat brooding. He'd never been able to feel angry with Humbert Daal—Humbert had been with him when they sneaked in to get a glimpse of Earth after the Destruction, and God knew that had been enough to scramble *anyone's* attitudes.

Humbert's poem *Epitaph for a Fool* had come out of that grim visit. Some of the surviving men might sneer at poetry, but John didn't think any of them would forget the lines, as long as their minds lasted:

> Recall not Earth, nor weep. We gelded waifs,
> We motes of Death cast on impassive seas,
> Own not the right of petulant protest
> Nor lien of mercy on the Pleiades.
>
> The worm, the flower, crisped in mega-blast,
> Sought not their fate. Yet, was it crueler shock
> Than trout-on-hook? Than gut-shot-bison-cow?
> Who wailed extinction of the pigeon-flock?
>
> Take steel for sod, take tungsten for its light,
> Take tinted glass for sky, and pipe for vine.
> Quaff tisanes for the crying of your loins.
> Recycled air your breeze, ship's grog your wine.
>
> Go swaggering up the starlanes, grinning, cursing,
> Deal blows to weaker creatures that you find.
> Run when you must, but not too far; and always
> Leave tales of might and daring deed behind.
>
> And when you're senile and you dare to sleep,
> You'll have invented lies enough to keep,
> And you'll not weep.

The small unarmed ship broke out of its short zeroing-in hop within easy radio range of Jessa. John waited a minute until the companion vessel, piloted by Luis Damiano, broke out a few miles away. Then he sent a call: "This is Unarmed Class Four Explo Ship *Council Bluffs*. John Braysen commanding. Is Humbert Daal available?"

There was a moment of silence, then the hum of a carrier wave. A bit of static distorted it. He heard a chopped-off syllable, then a mutter of hasty side-talk. Finally, "John? Commodore Braysen? This is Fred Coulter. How are you, sir?"

"Fred! Hello, hello! I'm okay—how are you?"

"Fine, John! Who's with you?"

"Don Bunstill's with me; and aboard *Mineola*—which should just be a separate blip on your radar screen—are Luis Damiano and Jim Cameron. We came light-handed. . . . Is Humbert Daal handy? And if not, can someone else give us permission to land?"

An embarrassed pause. "Hum's not here right now, Commodore—but for God's sake, come on down!"

"Thanks, Fred. The settlement's grown since I was here. I see a cluster of shacks just off the edge of a hill that seems to have big trees on it. There are level fields—Jessa flax, I guess—with a road running through them to the shacks, and a small clearing to one side of the shacks. Is that you?"

Coulter chuckled. "Yes. That's all the spaceport we've got, Commodore—we send our fiber by cart to one of the other alien compounds for sale. Just try not to land on the shacks."

"All right. Thanks. *Council Bluffs* and *Mineola* coming down on gravs."

Eight of the men on Jessa were clustered around. Coulter, flushed with pleasure and excitement, stammered introductions. "This is Walter Bain, Commodore—remember him? And Carl Muntz, and Joe Pina . . ."

John, knowing that he too was flushed, gripped the hands and mumbled remembrances.

But there was an awkwardness about any mention of Humbert Daal, until Coulter finally blurted out, "Hell— there's no sense in putting it off. The thing is, Hum's narked out right now. I mean, he's, well, sleeping off a hard jag. He's been hitting the drug pretty heavily lately."

John tensed, forced his face to stay calm. "That's too bad. Is he . . . How's his health?"

Coulter shrugged nervously. "We think okay. But lately he's getting more and more despondent. It's not a drug that's supposed to be harmful, but . . ."

John's own voice sounded odd to him. "They're all harmful eventually, one way or another." He resisted an impulse to put his hands in his pockets. *Damn it,* he thought irritably, *the stain's gone long ago.* "What's he been using?"

"*Dron.*"

Humbert Daal—who, when so moved, could scream the most numbing, daggerlike kind of invective—could also be the most gracious of companions. He was in the latter countenance now. "I can't begin to try to apologize, Commodore. I understand thoroughly how you must despise such depravity as the use of drugs."

John felt his face color. But he'd steeled himself for this. What was bothering him more was the almost irresistible effort of his eyes to turn again and again to the pair of sleek dainty animals huddled together in timorous watchful silence in the farthest corner of the room.

Daal didn't look too unhealthy. He'd gone to fat (shockingly, if one remembered his tigerish leanness of eight years ago). His thighs as he slumped in linenlike pajamas on the big overcushioned couch, were gross things, his belly a flaccid blob. But his skin was smooth, aglow with seeming health, and his eyes were the same pale, innocent blue. There was no redness of the eye whites, no dilation of the pupils, no puffiness of the lids. *Dron's* effects, at least until the advanced stages, were inward.

A movement in the corner drew John's eyes, despite his

resolve. One of the two creatures (could you call them humanoid?) was daring to move. It uttered a soft, mewing sound. It's limpid brown eyes, fixed on John, could have been an artist's symbolization of fear.

Humbert said to it gently, "Come on, my dear. He won't hurt you."

A moment more the creature hesitated, then with a sudden rush it ran to the couch and threw itself against Daal, to clutch at him, hiding its face, muttering in fright. A moment later, as if terrified of being left alone, the second one joined it.

They were both female, of course, and diminutively humanoid. They were the most advanced animal species on the planet, called the "jess," the planet taking its name from that. They *were* beautiful creatures, with the softest, sleekest of fur, pale cream except for a slightly darker shade along the spines and atop the head. What skin showed (the palms of their hands and the soles of their feet) was like a baby's. But their forms were not infantile; these two were definitely voluptuous; and John felt stirrings of lust which angered and embarrassed him.

Daal was chuckling. "You always *were* more of a prude than a fighting man ought to be, John. Yes, of course, these are my little love beasts. Is that so terrible? There were far worse perversions among the men you commanded, Commodore—even before we had the supreme excuse for whatever perversion each of us might choose. And what sort of perversion, Commodore John Braysen, impelled us to confine combat duty to one sex? Women fought in many of our internecine wars on Earth. Wouldn't it be more pleasing to you now if we'd had women alongside us?" He paused, smiling at John with those innocent blue eyes. "Was it some sort of prudery? Or was it a male jealousy, a masculine unadmitted realization of our inadequacy? Were we not punished by nature with the thoroughly civilized sentence of extinction?"

John couldn't suppress his trembling anger. "You damned sybarite! There *were* women, noncombatant specialists, aboard the capital ships. And for that matter, if you hadn't burrowed immediately into this sanctimonious non-belligerency of yours, you'd have seen that it's the norm, not the exception, among humanoids for the males to do the fighting. Hohdans, for instance—"

"Ah, yes, John; the Hohdans. I understand that even the most bloodthirsty of you—which, I grant you, *you* are not —finally became surfeited with slaughter and left the Hoh-dans."

John filled his lungs to shout some unthinking retort, but caught himself. There was no sense in a screaming quarrel with his host. "The Hohdans aren't monsters, Humbert. They meet their challenges, and have managed to survive. They expected us to want rehabilitation after our contract was finished. Anyway—"

Daal tittered, murmured, "Rehabilitation," and stroked his love beasts. They were over their fear of John now. Under Humbert Daal's caresses they began to stir sen-suously, to murmur like purring cats. One writhed itself to where it could lick at Daal's fat cheek with a delicate pink tongue. Daal said, in the friendliest of tones, "There's nothing bestial about them, John. They can learn to under-stand speech quite well, and even to use a few words. I'd put their intelligence closer to human than simian. And they're gentle—not like us. There's no malice in them, no viciousness. See—their teeth are vegetarian. And they're so clean . . . so utterly, sweet-smelling clean. . . ."

John almost retched with revulsion. "Thank you for the lecture!" He hesitated. But he'd best get along with it. . . . "What I came here for is something else."

Humbert smiled. "Yes, I know. Did you think you could ransack the whole sector for surviving men without the rumor reaching me? I'm surprised at you, John, falling for another pathetic little dream. Didn't you—didn't we all —pant after enough hoaxes when we were still insane with the shock of it?"

John told him quietly, "This time it's no hoax, Humbert. I've seen enough evidence to convince me."

Daal sighed exaggeratedly. "Getting senile so soon, John?"

John said, "Don't worry about whether I am or not—just consider the merits of the thing! If you thought there was a chance—even a tiny chance—wouldn't you join us? And wouldn't you persuade this little bunch of followers you have here to come along?"

For a minute Daal stared at him. One of the delicate female creatures gave a small pained cry, and John saw that Daal's fat hand was gripping it cruelly. An incredible thought occurred to him. "Well—would you?"

Suddenly the fat man laughed. "That's a funny question, Commodore. Of course I would. But I'll never let anyone take me on another wild-goose chase." He eyed John for a moment, and there was speculation in the pale blue eyes. "You'll have to bring me real evidence!"

Don Cameron, in *Mineola*, was gone to an upland lake about seventy miles away, where six other men were supposed to be camping.

"Commodore," Fred Coulter was saying, "I wouldn't have believed I'd ever lift off this planet again! But now I'm as excited as—"

John barely heard him. He was surreptitiously watching Humbert Daal and the four men who stood near him. Daal was smiling, chattering lightly of some other world where he'd been once; relaxed, oozing good nature. But there was a very faint slurring of Daal's syllables, and his smile came and went a little too easily. John recognized the symptoms. Daal had had a little chew of *dron* to soothe his nerves.

And the four with Daal (all of them, unprompted by Daal, had scoffed passionately at the possibility of live women) were too quiet—noticeably tense, if one watched them closely. And he'd seen more than one of them reach furtively to touch his loose shirt of slack-weave cloth.

Unobtrusively, he glanced in the direction of *Council Bluffs*. He was a good thirty yards from the ship. Daal and his four companions were closer to it, on the shorter side of a triangle—and they were in position to see into the open hatch.

Luis Damiano was fifty or sixty yards away, with the group of men other than Coulter who'd decided to join the departure. Luis wasn't armed, and there was no reason to suppose that any of the men with him were, either.

John had his pistol—a compact weapon that fired slim projectiles at high velocity—in the hip pocket of his undress trousers. The undress jacket, a zipper-front style, fit fairly snug but was of stretchable material, so he could get his hand under it and reach the hip pocket without too much delay.

But it was foolish, wasn't it, to suppose that Daal would try to seize the ship—or its intended passengers? Still, that little group definitely had something furtive in mind! And why had it positioned itself where it was?

By now Coulter, noticing John's abstraction, had stopped talking and was watching him curiously. Suddenly things moved in John's mind—the sort of hunches or guesses that made him the tactician he was. There'd been enough talk among Damiano, Cameron, Bunstill, and various of the local men for Daal to have pieced together a picture of the intended campaign, including that it would try to cast blame on the Vuls. And the Vuls might easily know there were men on Jessa. In Daal's thinking, at least, the result might be a vengeful Vul raid on Jessa.

And, within instants, John had decided what to do. He said quietly to Coulter, "Don't act surprised. Go get Damiano. Walk casually in that direction—but if I yell at you, run!"

He felt a quirk of annoyance at Coulter's bewildered look. "Damn it, man, be cool! And do as I say—bullets may start flying any instant!"

Coulter blinked once. But then his face went casual, he turned—without looking toward Daal—and walked away.

As soon as Coulter moved (all John wanted was to get him started away, to make a harder target), John turned. He got only two paces before Daal said sharply, "Stand still, Braysen!"

John turned, pretending surprise—and that turn, as he'd planned, put his gun pocket out of Daal's sight. He pretended to stare in astonishment at the pistol in Daal's hand. The other four had pistols out too—all comparatively clumsy bullet-firing weapons of medium caliber.

John could have smiled. The group was more than twenty yards from him. Daal was slightly fuzzed with *dron,* and the other four were definitely nervous. He couldn't have asked for better odds!

He had his hand on the pistol now. It came out smoothly and swept up to bear on his targets with the same motion. Two of their guns banged, and he could see the wildness of the aims. Humbert Daal was an instant getting over his surprise.

John didn't shoot to kill—but he didn't shoot *not* to kill, either. Just at the wrong moment, Daal turned his shoulders slightly, bracing his arm to shoot—which was fine if a man had time to do it. John didn't see where the slim bullet hit him; he was too busy dropping the four henchmen. He got them all in their shooting shoulders, with one slim bullet each, and they went down, dropping their pistols. He could glance away from them in time to see Humbert Daal collapse.

The needle bullet had evidently gone into the chest from the right armpit, and directly through the heart. The expression on the smooth fat face was astonished. Daal's left hand started tentatively up toward his chest. His right hand, still holding the pistol, sagged.

Then his eyes closed slowly, all expression left his face, his knees buckled, and the heavy bulk of him thudded to the ground.

John, feeling sick, walked slowly toward the prone group. He'd killed before—but not at close hand like this; not—not *men.* And Humbert Daal . . .

Damiano, Coulter, and the others ran up, their faces ludicrous. "Secure the ship," he told them dully, "and arm yourselves."

Council Bluffs, her distance hop completed, hung within radar distance of *Luna* and John's other fighting ships, waiting for *Mineola* to make a correction hop and appear alongside. Fred Coulter sat with him in the small control room.

Coulter said, "I'd never have dreamed he'd turn on us like that!"

John shrugged. "I guess he could see his whole existence in danger."

"Maybe," Coulter agreed. "We weren't willing to admit it, but I guess his mind was badly gone toward the last. In that worst bout with the *dron,* before he put himself to sleep entirely, he seemed to imagine he was back on Earth. Seemed to forget for a while that it had all happened. He turned out a poem that struck us as odd—we didn't know how far he'd drifted from reality. He knew his age, though. He gave the poem the title *Unbidden Lines at Thirty-Seven.*" Coulter smiled sadly. "His last poem, and he didn't even know where he was when he wrote it. At least, though, it wasn't as caustic as a lot of his stuff."

John said, meaning it deeply, "I hope it's preserved somewhere! If the human race survives—"

"Oh, it's preserved, all right. I've got all of his works in my baggage. I don't think I'd forget this last one for a while, anyway, even if it weren't written down." Coulter stared pensively at the deck for a moment, then began to recite:

The love of my life has long black hair.
Or am I sure? She may be blond!
No question, though—the love of my life is fair.

No hurry. There are oats to sow;
Wars to be won. No hurry.
If,
At times,
It may seem long—
Well, I'm still strong!

The painted mannequins pirouette by.
Their smiles more wooden grow.
Seasons more swiftly go.
My dear—
I fear!

John sat pondering glumly. "I guess," he said after a while, "we've all had periods when we tried to reject the reality of what happened to us." There were a couple of recent memories he'd like to reject right now. One was the innocent look of surprise on Humbert Daal's face as he died. The other was the bewildered, shattered weeping of Daal's two love beasts.

Coulter shifted indecisively in his chair, then suddenly looked at John. "Commodore, there's something I want to do right now, while I have the resolve. It's too useful to throw away—it's as good an anodyne as morphine. And, well, I've known it to save men from going completely off the deep end. But I'd rather not have it in my possession. I've taken it a few times, and—well, I want it put out of my reach!"

John's mouth suddenly felt dry. "What is it?" he asked hoarsely and unnecessarily.

Coulter took a small package from his pocket. The size of a man's little finger. . . . Wrapped in coarse brown paper, secured with a tiny dab of alien balsam. . . . John had no need to unwrap it to know how many *muzhees,* pea-sized lumps, of *dron* there were in the semitransparent length of plant stalk. Eight of them. Eight increments of ease, of forgetfulness, of any heavenly dream you wanted.

He took it with a trembling hand he hoped Coulter wouldn't notice. "I—I'll lock it up right now." And he did, before Coulter's eyes, in a little hand-weapon locker below the control console.

He wished Coulter would leave. Somewhere aboard there was a pint or so of two-hundred-proof ethanol. Mix it with a little water . . . It wouldn't kill the demanding thirst that gripped him, but it would ease it a little. . . .

(6)

JOHN LEANED toward *Luna*'s main control console and spoke into the pickup grille. "Thirty seconds to breakout!" He let his eyes follow the sweep second hand on the chronometer. He had the instrument recalibrated with Terran numerals. Twenty seconds. Fifteen. His hands were perspiring. There was always tension when a formation of ships tried to null over a long distance. A tiny error in computers or drives, or an exceptional anomaly in the little-understood fabric of null, could bring two or more ships into breakout in overlapping volumes of space. That would create unnatural high-molecular-weight elements. Two bodies might occupy the same space at the same time, but only for the nanosecond before spectacular disintegration.

Besides, even though this was their fourth raid, and the first three had been effective, in terms of their objectives . . . He trembled with an agonized doubt. In a real jam, when he had to come up with decisions and inspirations faster than his eyes could read data screens, would his mind work as of old? It didn't *feel* the same. They'd gotten through the first raids by virtue of good preplanning and the absence of any bad luck. But they hadn't avoided casualties completely. On the first raid they lost nobody. On number two, they'd lost four men, and another four lay in beds on Akiel. On the third raid they'd lost a ship (one of the Armed Scouts), with Don Bunstill and six other men aboard.

They'd captured two Bizh ships of approximately Medium Cruiser class, but those were on Akiel now, being rebuilt and refitted for humanoid crews, and wouldn't be available for a thousand hours.

Four seconds to breakout . . .

A klaxon bleated briefly. He felt the familiar instant's swirl of sensation, then starfields blossomed on the viewscreens.

Computer would be at work, shifting the ships back into perfect alignment. They were all okay. . . . His eyes moved from data screen to viewscreen to mass-detector globe, making sure formation was correct.

The klaxon bleated again.

"Launchers stand by!" he snapped into the pickup, even before he could see the pattern of the presumably enemy fleet. He darted glances at the lieutenants on either side of him, saw them punching computer keyboards. The only valid programming yet would be: "Arm defensive missiles; lock all ships into flagship control; pool sensors . . ." The klaxon cut itself down to a whisper. John could hear faint cross-talk on the common circuit. No one sounded excited. No reports of malfunction or unreadiness. He stared hard at the fuzzy blob on his centered radar screen. A dozen or more capital ships! How had they managed to get directly between him and the target?

Probability reckoning, of course—and right on the nose! He muttered a curse at himself. Too damned logical, those feints to one side and the other, the last two raids; then this try for the advance sector-command outpost. Well, he could run—null charge would be full in less than two minutes. He could just leave, without even wasting a salvo of missiles, which would be intercepted anyway.

But he'd put a lot of work into preparing this raid. And a familiar cool calculation was fermenting in his brain. The enemy blob was expanding slowly on the screen as he moved toward the target base.

Such a pitifully small striking force he had. . . .

But suddenly, compulsively, he was punching studs. "Null in eighty seconds!" he snapped into the pickup. "We're going to hop to just the other side of them; then hop again in a lateral expanding maneuver as soon as we're recharged. Defensive missiles only on the first breakout. On the next one, hit them centrally with every salvo we can fire. Forget the target! Then, as soon as we can, we're bagging for Rendezvous D, D for dog!"

The sweep hand trembled around. The program was all set. There'd be nothing for the skippers of the smaller ships to do, either, until they'd made the second short hop; then, if his ploy worked out, they'd be *busy*, making sure their computers didn't come up with idiot-genius defensive programs, watching out for malfunctions, coping with any emergency such as a serious near miss. He grinned tightly as the second hand started its last five tiny leaps. If the long chance went against them—a long one, but real—some of their own missiles might fight clear through the enemy defensive barrage and hit friendly ships.

Null! Breakout! No measurable time lapse for such a short hop. His eyes raced over instruments and screens. The Bizh fleet was no fuzzy blob now—it was a big cluster of multicolored blips on an aft radar screen, close, within easy missile range. He drew in a breath as dials told him just how close. If they wanted to pour maximum energy output into it, they could even aim rupters at him. And they had energy to use! He counted fifteen bright crimson blips that meant heavy cruisers.

He held his breath for long seconds, while his little fleet streaked in grav drive toward the star of the target planet —while the enemy kept pace. Then the enemy did just what he'd hoped. They nulled, without firing a missile, to put themselves once more between him and the target.

A few seconds after the blips vanished from the aft screens, they were on the forward screens again—this time a little out of fighting range. He punched at the keyboard, programming a few short grav-drive feints to keep them occupied. But he had no intention of trying to dodge past them; that would be senseless.

He was aware of the puzzled regard of the two lieutenants. "Look," he told them, "we'll be recharged eighteen or twenty seconds before they are. That's how long they lagged the last time. So, when we null, they'll be frantically wondering whether we'll go straight in toward the target or break out from some other angle. And when we break out instead in a circle around *them,* there'll be at least a few moments of confusion. They'll have to consider whether it might be a feint—with a whole fleet ready to hit the base from the opposite side. And while they're wondering, we'll be pouring in missiles. There'll be return fire—belatedly—but we'll fight that off until we're recharged. Then we'll leave without saying good-bye."

The lieutenants grinned doubtfully.

John waited, trying to forget the thirsty sensation in his mouth. Screens flared briefly and returned to normal—some missile the Bizh had lobbed toward him, a tentative feint or possibly even a challenge, routinely intercepted. He glanced at the dial. Most of a minute before null. The powerful enemy force could move toward him on grav drive, but in any game of tag he could move as fast as they could.

Thirty seconds to null. The lieutenants were tense now. He wondered if they realized that even now he was scoring in terms of the primary objective. The Bizh fleet could plainly see (even if they hadn't known) that the raiding ships were of Vul design—squatter cylinders than most, with all weapons ports in the curved sides, leaving the ends solid for a particular kind of grav shield.

But he was giving something away, too—or would be within seconds. They knew that he wasn't restricted to hitting bases. Also, he'd lost any chance to capture more ships.

Fifteen seconds . . . He felt wonderful, except for the thirsty sensation; almost relaxed. His talent hadn't deserted him! He let his hand hover over the null stud. . . .

Null! Breakout!

Seconds ticked by before the enemy reacted at all. Then the cluster of blips on laterally aimed radar screens exploded apart. But pulling power as they were would rob rupter beams and laser clusters! He felt a jar as a heavy salvo blasted away from his flagship; grinned at the startled lieutenants. "We're not wasting power counteracting

every little tremor—we're pouring it all into null charge!"
He glanced at the chronometer. Over three minutes to go.
. . . The screens began to flicker as some of his missiles
converged on the still too bunched enemy and were intercepted. Then an intense flash as a complex pattern saturated the defense and broke through. He darted a look at a
screen. "We got a big one!" More flickering, more spar-
ring between his offensive missiles and the enemy defensive
ones. Another blinding flare! The screens stayed dark for
a second, then came on as automatic overload switches
closed again. One of the lieutenants was swearing almost
hysterically now. Bright flares—because they were close
—enemy missiles being intercepted not far away. He was
sweating profusely, having second thoughts about his pug-
nacious action. The ship shuddered, and he went tense.
Had they gotten a hit? No—gunnery was using *Luna*'s
rupters to fight off enemy salvos. God! They were coming
in thick now! The screens were blanked out almost perpetually. Fifty-five seconds to null, even if the power drain
for defense didn't get any heavier. He leaned toward the
general intercom, listening to the babble of orders, curses,
and jubilant laughs. He punched a stud, stared at data that
scrolled across a screen: "Null time at present rate of
charge, forty-two seconds . . . forty-one seconds . . ."
His breath was coming hard now. Had he misjudged
things? He leaned forward again. "Gunnery!"

"Sir?"

"How many heavy missiles do we have left?"

"Nineteen. There aren't any good targets anymore!"

"Send them out, unarmed, in a tight bunch, slow, toward
the major source of this stuff that's after us!"

"Yes, sir!" Internal compensation was on now, of
course, with the need to be dodging; still he could feel the
jar, faintly, as the salvo blasted away.

And then there was nothing left to do but sit there,
trying not to cringe, while the chronometer made its painfully slow walk toward the red arrow. He knew, without
having to study the data screens, that the enemy's fury
would all be concentrated on *Luna* now—the much smaller

mass of the other ships wasn't nearly as good a target for homing missiles as she was. Six seconds . . . The screens blind with flares as all weapons fought desperately to intercept the swarm of incoming missiles. . . .

Null.

John sat limp and drenched with sweat in the pilot's seat. In that hell of nuclear warheads and raw energy they'd just left, the communications lock-in had been almost nonexistent. He wouldn't know until breakout at Rendezvous D whether the small ships had gotten away—or whether his clever, conceited pugnacity had cost more human lives.

God, how he wanted a *muzhee* of *dron*.

(7)

LISA DUVAL, Sixth Eldest (or possibly, she thought worriedly, now Fifth Eldest), skirted the last clump of tinkle bush and trotted toward Firstcamp. The short grass was soft and moist under her bare feet. In one hand she carried her eighteen-inch thicket bow and two arrows. In the other she clutched her kill—a two-pound creature like a very plump lizard with downy tan fur.

One of the younger girls saw her coming and called out in a preadolescent voice, "Lisa's back! Lisa's back!" A cook, a woman about a year younger than Lisa, came casually to the opening of the kitchen stall to see what game she was bringing back, looked disappointed, then smiled and shrugged.

Lisa pulled up, breathing hard, and handed the *krink* to the cook-woman. "Where's Eldest?"

The cook-woman, seeing that something was wrong, blinked worriedly for a moment. "She's down helping gather sugarcorn, I think. Why? What's happened?"

Lisa told her, "I think Ruby Weiss is gone!" She left the woman staring and ran downcreek.

Jane Ferris—Eldest, for the last year and a half—heard her call and came to meet her, carrying a bag that bulged with acorn-sized things. "What's wrong, honey?"

Lisa paused to get her breath. "I met one of the clan of chubbies upcreek. It said a woman went by last night, walking with her head down. She didn't have a bag, or a bow, or even a staff. It described her as the one with the narrow shoulders."

48

Jane's face seemed to age suddenly. "I was afraid of that, when she didn't show for breakfast."

Lisa said unbelievingly, "But she's not that old! I mean —I saw her three or four times in the last day or so, and she didn't seem in the least despondent. And she's never— There hasn't been any gossip. . . ."

Jane took her arm gently. "We've got to get a posse together! She may stop before she gets to the hole!"

Lisa hurried to keep pace. "But do you really think—"

"Yes, dear, I do. She was aging faster than most of us. I saw the signs, but never mentioned it to anyone. When you've been through it—"

"But—" Lisa broke off, surprised at her own sudden irritation. "I'm not anywhere near it yet. Seventeen or eighteen years, if I'm average!"

"Of course." Jane turned her head to smile gently. "And when it happens, you won't be the kind who goes to pieces. It doesn't mean a woman is really getting old at all. It's just a temporary upset, with your body chemistry changing, and if you keep your head you feel as well as ever in no time at all."

They ran on. Saffron-colored tinklebushes along the creek made their tinny sound as the brittle waferlike leaves rubbed together in the faint circulation breeze. They came into sight of the camp. Women and girls were milling about and acting frightened.

Eldest called out severely, "Here, now! Stop acting like a clan of hysterical chubbies! We've got to bring Ruby back, that's all. Freda, Mary, Eloise! Get your staffs and long bows. Bring enough sugarcorn and pemmican for several days." She turned to the cook-woman who'd talked to Lisa. "Nancy, you take Freda's place looking after the young girls while we're gone. Stay close to one another, and no hysterics! Do you hear me?"

Several of the women nodded slowly. One of the youngest girls—hardly eight years old—was sobbing. Jane went to her and put an arm around the thin shoulders. "Now, honey, stop that. Everything's going to be all right. Be a big girl for us! Okay?"

The child made an effort to stop crying, and nodded her head without opening her eyes.

Chubbies were mainly nocturnal, but there were usually a few ambling about a clan area. Lisa, who'd been in her teens when seized along with a thousand other women just before the devastation of Earth, remembered beavers; and she thought of chubbies as a kind of very large, evolved beavers, though, of course, from some planet far from the Solar System. Very fat beavers.

A full-grown male chubby might weigh sixty pounds in this environmental segment, which had a gravity of about one gee. They were gray-furred and had teeth suitable for beaverlike activity. The chubbies' intelligence, she thought, was almost of human level, though there were differences in the *kind* of intelligence.

This clan occupied a low hill on the left bank of Home Creek. Burrow openings all had little canopies of interwoven brush shoots to keep out rain. Beneath several of these canopies sat chubbies, silently watching the women trot along the creekside trail.

The women were past the hill, and skirting around clumps of tinklebush, before they met the old female who spoke the best English. She approached timidly as they stopped. "Please, women? Give I truths?"

Jane murmured to the other women that they might as well take a breather anyway. Lisa sank gratefully to the cool grass. Jane reached out a hand, and the chubby reached out a paw, and they touched in ceremony of neighborliness. "Thank you, good neighbor," Jane said.

The female chubby squatted, seeming to become a furry ball. "Sorry I, tall neighbors, that one of you has gone. Husband mine saw her small time before light. Sent he two young males to give her help if any Large Beasts offer fangs. But she see them, and say, 'No, no, thank you; but you go home.' "

Jane asked a little urgently, "How far did they follow her?"

"Half of way to Large Wall."

"Did she stay near the creek?"

"For small way, not more. She cross creek and go half to side around curve, half to Large Wall. Husband mine think she go to hole like other sick women."

Jane sighed and got to her feet. "Thank you, good neighbor. Are there reports of Large Beasts along the creek lately?"

"Seeing of Large Beasts, not in twelve lightings. But we not go more than halfway to Large Wall."

"Thank you," Jane said again.

They found Ruby's tracks, crossed the creek to follow them, and angled to the side. There was no more talk until the next stop for breath. Then Mary said glumly, "That's seven of us gone now."

Jane gave her a frown. "Ruby's not gone yet!"

Freda, who hadn't spoken one word on the trip, burst out almost hysterically, "When has anyone come back from the hole? Four—*four*—have gone into it, and all we've ever found was corpses half-eaten by animals. We ought to fill up the hole!"

Jane said sharply, "Hush! Don't scream like that!" But after a minute she said, "Maybe we will fill up the hole. I thought, when Jenny went, that she'd be the last." She was silent for a moment. "But even if we did, any more of us who went off the deep end could just wander off into a wild area. We've got to work out something more. We have to begin holding talk fests or something, to help anyone who feels that way." She glanced at Lisa (who was the only one of the posse still of child-bearing age).

Mary said sullenly, "What does it matter, anyway? Why don't we *all* just go through the hole, or find some other way to die, and get it over with? How's it going to be for the younger girls, having us drop off one by one until there's no one who can remember what a sky looked like, or that some trees on Earth grew three hundred feet tall? And what a man looked like." She ignored Jane's angry look. "And when all but the youngest are gone—how's it going to be for *them?* Imagine four or five old crones trying to gather food and defend themselves against the predators that have come through the hole. Imagine the last one—alone!"

Jane said scornfully, "I guess we may as well stop right here and have supper. Food always makes you feel better, Mary."

When they'd gotten the fire going, the Eldest said firmly, "The last ones can make their own decision. That'll be a long time yet—we're still a vigorous community. We're happy, aren't we, most of the time? Didn't you see the young girls playing tag along the creek this morning, laughing just as if they were ordinary children on Earth? Doesn't the artificial light feel as warm on your skin as the sun did? Doesn't a sandwich taste just as good here?"

Mary laughed bitterly. "No. I can't laugh more than one bleat without asking myself what the hell I'm laughing about." She met Lisa's eyes. "You, virgin—maybe you can dream that some miracle is going to impregnate you so that you'll have something to use those cute breasts of yours. But when you go through the change, you won't dream anymore. Because even if—"

Suddenly Eloise was crying silently and Freda was screaming. Jane surged to her feet, bent over Freda, and slapped her hard, back and forth, back and forth. "Shut-up! You weakling!"

When things were quieter, Jane said tersely, "Being half-alive is better than being dead. And men were exasperating at times—oh, so exasperating! Wasn't love ninety percent illusion, anyway? A few moments of ecstasy now and then, and long hours of futile anger at some clod's thoughtlessness or actual cruelty. It seems to me that as long as we last we ought to show a little dignity. The chubbies must think we're a ratty bunch, going around wailing. And one of us, now and then, plodding off to die like—like some sick rodent!" She motioned them to their feet. "We'll go another two miles before we sleep."

Lisa lay on her back staring up at the other arc of the segment. It was quite dusky on this side now, but a ring of fires kept away predators. In another hour the trek would resume, and then they'd be carrying torches for the same purpose.

How little they knew of this utterly alien place where they lived!

This segment's extent and overall shape could be seen easily enough. It was simply a cylinder. The dimensions had been paced off (and in the first year of residence, or captivity, some of the older women had fashioned crude transits of sticks). From wall to wall was a little over thirty-seven miles. Those walls were flat and parallel. Diametrically across the cylinder, to the opposite arc, was about eighty-five miles.

The light source was a hub (looking wand-thin from here) that stretched from wall to wall along the axis of the cylinder. Light shone from one side of it at a time, changing slowly as if the hub rotated on the same axis in about nineteen hours. That made the "day" and "night" (though the latter was never really dark, because of light from the opposite, daylit, arc). Seasons were created by a movement of the brightest part of the hub from end to end.

Some of the women who'd been educated on Earth thought that the gravity was caused by a rapid though undetectable rotation of the whole segment. But if that were true, why did the mountains pile up along both walls, while the low meadows were in the middle—along with the "ocean" into which rivers flowed from both ends? Undoubtedly, Lisa thought, it was artificial gravity, though nobody here claimed to know much about that.

Clouds, when there were any, hung not more than a mile or two above the curved land. That was obvious, because when it was clear on this side (or wherever around the curve you went) and cloudy on the other side, the top of the clouds looked just as far away as the unclouded land. A really cloudy night could be frighteningly dark, with just a faint luminosity from overhead.

Of course, if one remembered that a number of small spaceships had brought them here, and that strange creatures called Chelki had piloted the ships and cared for the women, one didn't forget that this was some sort of a pen. And that implied that the Chelki—or those humanoids called Vulmoti, who ruled the Chelki—might return anytime. But both the Chelki and the Vulmoti were associated with some vague horror, and one didn't talk about them, especially before the younger girls.

Some of the women had developed strange ideas about this place, but Lisa thought of it as fairly reliable and self-tending. There must be some circulation of air other than that caused by day and night and seasons. There must, therefore, be openings somewhere—perhaps in that central hub from which the light came. And there must be some hole beneath the "ocean" from which water was drained—obviously evaporation couldn't account for more than a small fraction of the rain that replenished the rivers, via the brooks in the mountains.

But none of the women had seen where they entered this segment.

It was fairly certain, she thought, that the segment had never been intended to have any interconnection with other segments—not through the walls, anyway. The hole must have been made by some kind of accident.

Something—a meteorite, conceivably—had struck the wall toward which they were trekking, just about at the highest point of the mountains. But that height changed from time to time, obviously, because there were clear signs that erosion went on steadily, but was counteracted by something that pushed the mountains up from underneath.

The hole, apparently, had been covered with dirt (on this side of the wall, at least). But gradually the dirt had washed away—a ravine slanting down from the hole showed that. And, with the hole exposed, rain then started to wash the remaining dirt through into the next segment (which was a strange place with dimmer and different-colored and longer days), until the entire hole was open. It wasn't big—just a ten-foot hole in the metal of the wall, a thick oval, with ragged edges as if the metal had rusted through (though the metal of the wall was nonrusting and far stronger than steel).

Beasts had come through that hole. But they didn't spread throughout the segment, probably because the air smelled different in here. A steady mild breeze blew out of the hole, bringing that other smell with it. And the beasts seemed to come only so far as that smell persisted. That influx of foreign air felt drier, too.

The chubbies said the hole had opened up only several of their generations ago. But that was long before the women had found it.

No one knew how the notion of going into the hole to seek death had started. But it had—and now Ruby was the fifth to follow it.

Jane's voice startled Lisa out of her reverie. "Time to be moving, girls!"

The rain-washed ravine led up to the summit at this point—less than twenty yards from the wall—then slanted toward the jagged hole in the thick metal.

Ruby's footprints showed in the mud.

They paused to peer through the hole. It happened to be full night in the other segment also; but as there were no clouds there, ever, the reddish twilight was adequate for walking down the slope from the hole. The breeze in their faces had a sharp, acrid smell—and a tinge of carrion. Mary asked in a hushed voice, "Why don't we take torches?"

"Because," Jane told her, "we don't have three hands apiece." They all had their bows slightly drawn.

In single file, they stepped through.

This bare slope obviously consisted of dirt washed through from their own side. At the top, it was still moist, but a few yards down, the dry air had eliminated that. The soil was loose and slippery.

At the bottom, fifty yards from them, was the natural summit of these foreign hills. There was no grass, but gnarled, russet-leaved spreading trees formed an almost solid cover over the descending ground. They picked their way down the bare slope, having to use their staffs to keep their footing. At the edge of the grove Jane whispered, "Let's give our eyes a few minutes to adjust."

Lisa peered ahead. The light was disturbing; for one thing, it made the other women's faces look strange. She tested her bow, making sure the arrow was properly nocked.

They started on down. She wanted to look back toward the hole now, even though trees hid it, but didn't.

Jane, leading, stopped. There was vague movement to one side, in the gloom.

Then there was a low, hesitant, gobbling sound.

From that moment, things happened so fast Lisa couldn't remember them all afterward. A dozen or more things, like flying blankets, launched themselves toward the women. Certainly not the Large Beasts—smaller, flatter of body, fast-moving. They came with low, deadly snarls, in long sailing leaps. Lisa frantically pulled her bow, let the one arrow fly, then dropped the now-useless weapon. She swung her staff up desperately to fend off the thing almost upon her. She had a quick, arrested impression of four legs extending to the sides, stretching a pair of flying membranes; of a flat body; of foreclaws outstretched toward her; of a pointed snout; of small but keen fangs in a gaping mouth; of tiny beady eyes. The thing was smaller than, say, a collie, but far more limber and agile than any canine. She saw these things as screams of the other women shrilled in her ears. And she was falling backward, trying to evade those reaching claws. She let herself slide down the slope as she tried to bring her staff into position again. She did do that—and felt the weight of the creature almost knock the staff from her hand. But it sent the creature sprawling. It righted itself, with a grunt of pain, and leaped away downslope. She heard Freda scream again. She struggled to get her footing; came to one knee; saw Jane grimly fighting off at least two of the things that had hold of her; threw herself in that direction and poked one of them viciously with her staff. It squalled and leaped down the slope. She saw another launching itself at her from the side; barely managed to twist her body, get the staff pointed toward the beast, and plant the butt against the ground. The animal impaled itself on the staff. She tried once to shake it off, but couldn't, so she dropped the staff and leaped toward Jane, who was flat on her back punching and clawing at a couple of the things atop her. Lisa grabbed one and simply lifted it and smashed it to the ground. It flopped, squalling, then writhed away. She got a one-handed grip on the one still clinging to Jane, but it decided suddenly to join its fellows in retreat, and jerked away from her. She whirled. Freda was face down, sobbing, but Mary was on both knees, her staff held firmly across her chest, a vicious look on her face. Two dead creatures lay near her, in addition to the one still impaled, and now motionless, on Lisa's staff. Eloise was on her feet, staff ready. She looked dazed.

But the attack was definitely beaten off.

The women all gathered around Jane. She was a mass of ugly, gashed wounds. She lay quietly on her back, face up, eyes wide open, breast heaving.

Then, in the dim light, Lisa saw that blood pumped awfully from Jane's left thigh. Lisa was on her knees immediately, tearing off her own blouse for bandages. But Jane made a weak movement of her hand and said hoarsely, "No, don't touch me—just let me lie still. My . . . abdomen is ripped open too."

Mary exploded, "Jane!"

Jane shuddered, closed her eyes in pain, then opened them again. She seemed hardly able to see at all. "Lisa . . ."

"Yes, honey! I'm here!"

"Lisa, you're . . . You must be leader now."

For a moment Lisa misunderstood her, thinking she only referred to the trek home. Then she cried out, "No, Jane! You're—you'll be all right! And—and anyway, Mary is next oldest!"

Jane sighed shudderingly and squeezed her eyes shut again. "No . . . You—have ne-necessary traits. I want you . . . all th-three of you . . ."

And that was the last Jane ever said.

The four of them stood there staring at one another. Lisa was having a hard time to control sobs. "I'm not," she got out, "not—old enough. . . ."

Mary came and put a rough arm around her shoulder. "Yes you are, too! And as she said, you're the one. The rest of us here are all quite a few years older—but there's something wrong with each of us. Now—shut up! That's the way it's going to be. I'll help you—all of us will help you. Shut up!"

And nothing Lisa could sob out would change Mary's mind, nor Freda's, nor Eloise's.

Each of them had minor wounds, but no serious ones. They did what bandaging was practical, then used their staffs to dig out a grave for Jane. There were rocks enough, a little way farther down the slope, to make a cairn. Eloise protested, at first, that they ought to try to carry the body home; but Mary had the clinching argument for that: "No. The fewer graves we have around for the younger girls to see, the better."

They found Ruby's body where the band of gliding creatures had been feeding on it. Freda and Eloise were sick, and Mary looked as if only stubbornness kept her from being sick too, and Lisa only just managed, somehow, to control her stomach. They put what was left of Ruby in another grave close to Jane's. They lashed together a pair of crosses out of Jane's staff and longbow and muttered whatever prayers seemed to have any meaning. Then they started "home."

(8)

JOHN STARED GLUMLY at the intercom grille for several minutes, then reached out and pressed one of the studs below it.

A voice said, "Communications."

"Damiano," John said, "I want a radio beam to each of the other ships, just strong enough to reach them without carrying too far beyond. There's no telling who or what might be within range of a broadcast. Can you handle that?"

"Well, yes, Commodore. It'll take a little while, though, if we have to lock onto all of them initially by telescope. Maybe half an hour."

"Go ahead." John sighed. "I don't think we ought to risk using radar. And while you're at it, aim the telescope at Number Four again. If there's anyone alive aboard, they may have gotten some visual signal rigged up by now."

"We've already done that, sir—I was just about to call you. Not the faintest light from her."

"All right." John got restlessly from his seat, glanced with unreasonable annoyance at the two lieutenants, who watched him in somber silence, and left the control room. Damage Control said that whatever patching up had to be done outside *Luna* was progressing well, but he wanted to go to Engineering and see for himself, on the special screens they'd rigged.

After that he made a brief tour of the ship, talking to Gunnery (who had no problems, except that they were nearly out of missiles of all classes) and to Stores (who said there'd be no food problem if they got back to Akiel

59

or someplace within three hundred hours). Then he went back to the Control Room to talk to his meager fleet.

"This is the commodore. I'm afraid we have to assume that Number Four is completely dead. She nulled on comps, but hasn't communicated, moved, or shown a light since. We're going to close in on her now, and if there's no bad radioactivity, board her. If any of you have any problems, keep them until we're in a tight group, when we can exchange weak radio messages. Some of you may show an object or cluster of objects on your mass detectors in direction twenty-eight by six by thirty-one, distance one-third of a million miles. We barely have it on ours. Probably only a stray comet or a cluster or rocks, but we won't take chances. Close in on *Luna* at will."

Ten hours later the mutilated corpses off Number Four were in *Luna's* infirmary, and a crew in spacesuits was at work patching Number Four's hull. The hole was ironically small. But it had been made by a bit of high-velocity steel from some detonation, which had ricocheted around inside and achieved total slaughter. No radioactivity, no rupter shaking, no heat beams—just that deadly chunk of steel, a ten-thousand-to-one chance penetration; and eight more men were gone.

The object at a third of a million miles had turned out, after cautious scouting, to be a typical mass of cometary material adrift in this sparse, dark region between galactic spiral arms. But that didn't make John feel any better. Eight more men gone! And Vez Do Han might want him to make additional raids on the Bizh. John wouldn't know how many until he nulled back to rendezvous with the Hohdan.

His insides churned with bitter guilt and self-doubt. He'd felt so confident, so utterly assured, when the idea for that encircling action had flashed into his mind. Hadn't it been, actually, criminal foolhardiness?

He got up from his bunk, where he'd been sitting for an hour staring dully about his quarters, and wandered into the small office compartment. His eyes went uncontrollably to the locked safe in one corner. "No!" he snarled furiously, and swallowed without ridding himself of the thirst-that-was-not-thirst.

But why, when he brought that small packet of *dron* aboard *Luna* from *Council Bluffs,* had he locked it in his office safe? Why hadn't he taken it to Infirmary for the medic to keep?

He leaned against the edge of the hatch, dizzy, wondering if he were going to be sick. "Damn it!" he growled. "That stray hit wasn't anything I could have foreseen!"

But *was* he the battle commander he'd once been? Certainly he'd felt fine—but any blundering fool felt fine before he made his clumsy mistakes. Shouldn't he have nulled away at once, avoiding the fight completely? Tangling with whole Bizh fleets was no part of his arrangement with Vez Do Han.

Twenty men lost, in four insignificant raids. Not only a terrible fraction of all the men left alive—but men he knew. Comrades-in-arms.

Bart Lange should have left him on Drongail.

He turned and pounded a fist against the steel bulkhead. What an egomaniacal fool! He swallowed hard, drew in a ragged breath.

And then, trembling, cursing himself, he turned and walked slowly, defeatedly toward the safe.

John stirred lazily in his bunk. What was that sound? He recalled vaguely that there was something he ought to do. . . . Oh, yes . . . it was the intercom. He turned his face toward it. "Hello. Who is it?"

"Engineering, sir. Emergency repairs to all ships are complete."

"Oh. Well . . . that's good."

There was a pause, then the voice, sounding puzzled, asked, "Are we nulling soon, sir?"

"Nulling?" John thought that over. Of *course* they could null, anytime he felt like it. He was commanding the fleet, wasn't he? He chuckled, then yawned. "I don't think we'll go anywhere for a while yet. There's no hurry. Tell everyone to relax and be comfortable, will you?"

There was another silence. Finally the voice said doubtfully, "Yes, sir."

John rolled onto his side, wiggled himself into a comfortable position, and let drowsiness stalk him as it might. He felt wonderful. There'd been something worrying him, some anxiety or other about decisions he'd made that had cost several men. That was too bad—but everyone died sooner or later, didn't he? And to die gloriously in a battle —quickly, without any prolonged suffering—wasn't bad at all. He hoped *he'd* die that way, whenever the time came. Unless, of course, he could arrange just to sleep, and slip away without knowing it at all.

He felt wonderful! Why had he so perversely denied himself *dron* for so long? He'd been very foolish. . . .

"John! John! Wake up!"

John rolled onto his back, worked at raising his languid eyelids, and peered up at whoever was shaking him. "Oh —Bart. How are you?"

Bart stared down at him, mouth a grim line. "That, eh? How much did you have, and how long ago?"

John pushed himself into a sitting position. He yawned. "I've got to have a shower, then something to eat. Oh. How much did I have, you ask? Just a *muzhee*. A pellet the size of a pea. If there were any peas anymore." He chuckled. "Stop looking at me like a dean of men! I'm all right—I'm fine! Test me—ask me the multiplication table, or the decimal logarithm of three! Ask me to recite our roster. Aaron—Anders—Baker—Bunstill—" He broke off. "Oh. We lost Bunstill, didn't we?"

Lange growled an obscenity. "Yes, we lost Bunstill. And we've lost nineteen others in five raids. But this last time we gave a Bizh fleet a real clobbering! We've fulfilled our obligation to Hohd, or most of it, and we're a fighting unit again. There are almost two hundred of us left, John—and we've got our job to do! Are you going to yellow out and go back to that infant medicine?"

John frowned mildly. "You don't understand *dron*, Bart." He sighed. "I guess we'd better be nulling to our rendezvous with Vez. Are you going back to your own ship right away? If not, will you stop in at my Control Room and give the orders—"

Lange snarled, seized him by the shoulders, and hauled him to his feet. "Damn it, John, you're the commodore! Even more than ever, after this last battle, the men look up to you as just about half-god! Don't let them see you limp and—and spineless like this!"

John sighed again. "I'll tell you, Bart, I don't want to be any part god. But I suppose you're right." He bent to pick up his jacket from the floor, where he'd evidently let it fall. "We'll null as soon as you're aboard your own ship."

Vez Do Han said, "Yes, it *is* disturbing that they were able to predict so accurately where you would strike on the fourth raid." He made a palms-down gesture of foreboding. "It bespeaks acuteness on their part. And I am sorry you lost a crew. That, in view of your generalship —which was once more demonstrated!—was plain bad luck. But I feel, John Braysen, that we had better not ask you to raid again in that general area. I am thinking that a very brief strike or two at some base elsewhere would be wiser. Say, far out along the spiral arm, beyond the bulk of their empire. A strike there could not be construed as direct interdiction of their moves against our allies, who, by the way, report gratifying effects." He rubbed his furry cheek. "The prime purpose, after all, is not to damage bases, but to make trouble, if we can, between the Bizh and the Vulmoti. The distant strikes I suggest will better fit that purpose now."

John said, "A campaign that far away will call for some reconnoitering."

"Yes, it will require some hopping about. I have been thinking—could you not use a rendezvous somewhere near the edge of the Vulmotean Empire? The timing, then, of your appearance at various spots would force the Bizh to think in that direction."

John suppressed a sigh. "We would have to start absolutely loaded with munitions, fuel, and food. Are you prepared to supply the first two? Food we can get at Akiel."

"We are prepared to do so, yes—but only over a period of some hundreds of hours. Assembling and moving such a large stock would attract the attention of spies. You still have two Bizh ships being refitted on Akiel—wherever that is. By the time they are ready, we will have gotten together your missiles and fuel wire at some little-visited place."

John's mind raced. He'd been thinking with longing of the Klee ship the Omniarch had promised him. Aside from its possibly fearsome potential in battle, it would provide almost as comfortable a base (if it were as big as claimed) as a planet. He could take his whole roster of men aboard at one time. But he couldn't tell Vez about that. . . . He said, "By the way, speaking of unvisited places, our welcome on Akiel has worn thin. At your last meeting and mine, we spoke of some uninhabited planet within the safety of your region that we might occupy. If you've chosen one, perhaps it can also serve as the depot where you assemble the munitions."

Vez's eyes fixed on him intently for a minute. "An excellent idea. I *have* chosen the planet. When would you like to examine it?"

"Not for several Hohdan days, if you will indulge me. I have a lot of refitting to get started, not to mention morale matters. May I dispatch a drone to your headquarters when I am ready?"

"By all means, friend John Braysen. Until next joining, then?"

"Until next joining, Vez Do Han."

John returned to Akiel and hastily looked up the Full Male Chelki. "I must get word to the Omniarch quickly. I'll null to wherever he wants me to meet him."

The Chelki eyed him expressionlessly, his four legs planted solidly, his head elevated to a level with John's. "As you can know, Co-mo-dore, my ancestor's location is not of knowledge to me. A message will go by routes not direct. I can not say how long it must travel. But I will send it at once."

(9)

BULVENORG, Second Prime Senior Marshal of the Defense
Perimeter of the Grand Empire of Vulmot, sat listening to
the gab and palaver and wrangling of the hastily assembled
symposium. Most of the officers here were his direct subordinates, but as usual he allowed them a period of free
rein. He listened as a concerned but unfrightened feline
might listen—slumped in his chair, eyelids drooped half-
shut, ears only occasionally flicking at some significant bit
of the babble.

Not that Bulvenorg was feline in body form. He was
humanoid, beyond any argument, even to the four thick
but deft fingers and one thumb on each capable-looking
hand. If the nails were even thicker and more firmly
rooted than a Hohdan's, that was because the Vulmoti had
evolved in a harsh environment. He could have worn a
man's shoes, of rather wide contour, even though the toes
in them would have been more prehensile than a man's. His
face would not have been mistaken for human—the planes
of the cheeks, widely separated just forward of the ears, converged toward the front so that his large nose, moderately
jutting chin, close-set eyes, and front teeth occupied too
narrow a space to be human. Those teeth were more
carnivorous than a man's, but not to the extent that a
Vulmot couldn't chew grain.

Bulvenorg was stocky, by human standards—an inch
over six feet, with an Earth-gee weight of a little more
than three hundred pounds. He was not fat, nor was he
musclebound. Most other humanoid species found it hard
to understand how a Vulmot could be so lithe and quick-

moving, so nearly double-jointed, so capable of relaxing all his muscles when he wished. But then, few humanoid species knew how Terran felines (while they still existed) could metamorphose instantly from limp somnolence to spring-steel action.

In that latter way Bulvenorg seemed feline.

His pointed, tufted ears began to twitch more frequently. He lifted a hand to brush at the short-cropped wiry black hair that grew above his sloping forehead (a slope that was compensated by a bulging skull farther back). A slow flush darkened his already tawny complexion. He was not angry, but impatience was creeping over him. The disorganized contention of small groups had ceased to scratch up any new information or ideas. He straightened in his chair.

At once, the officer who was chairing the symposium rapped on his lectern (Vulmotean chairmen never sat) with a pencillike thing that was, actually, a self-powered weak laser capable of little more than slightly charring a kind of paper adapted to the purpose. The amplified rapping brought the hall to instant attention.

Bulvenorg, reaching up a hand to press a stud on his uniform lapel, said in a low but silky voice, "It is clear that many of you are trying to disguise bafflement." He paused to allow a very brief moment of resentful grumbling. "The civilian delegate has indulged his biases by suggesting that units of one or another of our military organizations did, indeed, make gratuitous raids upon outposts of the Bizh Empire, for reasons, as he cutely puts it, that no sane individual could comprehend. Our Director of Public Relations has replied at length to that perhaps frivolous suggestion, lending it, I feel, more dignity than it deserves. Our Chief of External Intelligence has eloquently extolled the difficulties of spying within an alien empire many hundreds of light-years from our most remote borders, with whom we do not even have consular relation. And finally we have heard a report from my own adjutant, outlining steps we have taken against conceivable massive retaliatory raids by the Bizh." He paused again, looking for signs that any individuals were not yet talked out. Not that he couldn't steamroller over them, of course, but he preferred not to. He wanted to adjourn the symposium very soon without leaving anyone angry.

"It does strike me, though," he resumed, "that no one has even casually suggested that these mystifying raids—and we must not deny that our Intelligence is indeed working under extreme handicaps—are deliberately planned to provoke hostilities between us and the Bizh."

There were grunts of surprise and chagrin.

"That possibility, of course," he said, "was obvious from the beginning. I did not mention it because I hoped that someone had been considering it from different angles than I and would contribute his thinking. I now suggest that each of you ponder the idea and be prepared to discuss it at some possible future meeting."

The civilian delegate—an old adversary with whom Bulvenorg shared grudging mutual respect—cleared his throat. Bulvenorg looked at him, which was tantamount to offering him the floor.

The civilian said, "An interesting thought, especially from one who seldom bothers with such subtleties. Whom do you have in mind as possible perpetrators? Were you thinking of aliens, or were you wondering if somebody of our own felt a need for bugaboos, to ensure a continued flow of appropriations?"

Bulvenorg grinned. "Do not think that the possibility escaped me. However, as my job is the defense of empire and possessions, I went to considerable pains to make sure it was *not* some of our own people. And, indirect though our information may be, it is entirely clear that aliens—and a very small force, on the surface at least—are the 'perpetrators.' I thank you for supplying the word. I had been thinking of them in harsher terms."

The civilian bowed. "I find myself your ally in hoping to avoid such a war. Is it your intention—may we hope—may we *supplicate* that you will reveal the identity of these dastards?"

Bulvenorg let himself look frustrated and ruffled.

"That," he growled, "is what calls for desperate efforts on our part. And since we have no hint as yet—though I can think of several candidates—I see no point in further discussion at this time."

The civilian laughed the grunting Vulmotean laugh. Bulvenorg got to his feet and moved casually among the departing crowd, shaking hands here, offering amenities there. He did not really dislike this consorting with subordinates, but when, as now, it delayed him from vital activities, he had to try hard to hide impatience. Finally most were gone. He touched his microphone stud again and spoke to the chairman, still standing more or less patiently at the lectern. "Admiral Gusten, may I have a word with you?"

In his quarters, Bulvenorg got a bottle from his desk and poured small glasses of spirits for Gusten and himself, not spending much time on ceremony. It was a simple, businesslike liquor, about half-alcohol and half-water, with trace flavorings that gave it a slightly burned, slightly sour taste and smell. "I thought for a minute," he remarked, "that you were going to have to rap that fool civilian quiet."

Gusten grinned. "He's been a politician so long he knows before a chairman does when the chairman's about to reach for the pencil. Actually I thought, didn't you, that he was unusually agreeable?"

Bulvenorg made the thumb-to-forefinger sign of agreement. "He was here to needle us, for the sake of votes. . . . Has it occurred to you, Gusten, who's probably giving us this little ear singe?"

Gusten put thumb to little finger (negative). "I'm completely baffled! I can't imagine who'd be able to get hold of a dozen or more of our vessels—including one *nave*-class ship of forty thousand *lohm!* I didn't think we'd had that many captured in five generations."

Bulvenorg shrugged one shoulder and sipped a little of his drink. "That is a puzzle. Conceivably someone has built secretly to our design. An incredibly thorough job, if

so—every scrap of metal, every photograph, every magnetometer probe we've been able to lay our hands on or get
testimony about points to our own ships. I suspect we'll
have to unlock archives that no one's looked at for a
lifetime, to find records of ships actually lost." He sat
looking at his subordinate. "However, can't you think of
one species that would painstakingly acquire ship by ship
and hoard them for use against us?"

Gusten frowned. "Naturally, the longevity of our often-
puzzling slaves—the Chelki—occurs to me. I even did a
little research into that. The two minor rebellions, if you
could call them that, within a hundred Vulmot years didn't
result in any ships being taken and not recovered."

Bulvenorg smiled mirthlessly. "No. But there *have* been
ships lost with no explanation."

"Chelki technician genders," Gusten protested, "aren't
capable of that kind of violence!"

"Technician genders, no. But we've been unable to unravel the full puzzle knot of Chelki hormones. How do
we know that some Full Male somewhere, kept for breeding stock, hasn't worked out a way of developing individuals who *look* like neuters but have warrior instincts?"

Gusten looked startled. "Do you think that's possible?"

Bulvenorg gulped down the rest of his drink and waved
the glass impatiently. "It's just one thing that occurred to
me. Anyway, the ships may have been gathered together by
various devious routes—a coalition of our rivals, if you
want to be realistic, could probably amass such a total. The
more immediate question is, who's crewing them? They
run the risk of capture, or at least of having bodies
recovered little enough blasted to be identifiable; so it's
not any of the empires with whom we play *turg* and *miant*
from time to time. Can't you think of a small, fanatically
daring group of humanoids who hate us with every micro-
lohm of their being?" He watched his subordinate with
disappointment. "Even when you add the apparent genius
of that battle against a Bizh defensive task force?"

Gusten's mouth popped open. "You mean—the Terrans?
And Com—what was that silly rank designation—Commo-

dore John Braysen? Why, I didn't think there was more than a handful of them still alive, besides that overfat poet on some planet called Jessa. I thought Braysen died on—let me see—Drongail."

Bulvenorg showed his teeth in a not-quite-smile. "Braysen did drift as far as Drongail, and according to our reports, took to chewing *dron*. As for the rest of them—I did a little checking this morning. There might conceivably be as many as three hundred of them left. I've always wondered if that decision about them—to leave them alive as object lessons—wasn't imprudent as well as imhumane. Especially John Braysen. We should have made sure *he* was dead."

Gusten slowly sipped the rest of his drink and set the glass down. "I see your logic. But it's incredible."

"Incredible? Think deeper, Gusten. They were with Hohd for many *megashegs*. And the Bizh have been making *turg* eyes at two or three small empires between them and the Hohdan region. What would be more logical than for Hohd to try to convince the Bizh that *we* were interested in that advance?"

Gusten slowly touched thumb to forefinger. "Indeed! As perhaps we ought to be! Should the Bizh expand down that spiral arm, and eventually overcome Hohd—where else would they turn next, assuming continued expansionism, but across the Sparse Regions to *our* spiral arm? However, that is a long way in the future. I don't suppose we might consider launching a punitive campaign against Hohd."

Bulvenorg reached for the bottle and refilled the glasses. "Hardly. They are too strong—and with us badly weakened, even if we *could* win an all-out war with Hohd, the Bizh would top *turgs* in the whole galactic sector." He sipped. "We must counterplan, of course. And first we must make sure I'm right; after all, I offer only a tenuous chain of logic. First of all, we shall investigate Jessa—that fat poet and his few followers, though they foreswore all fighting, might know what is stalking the *miant*. And we shall send a ship to Drongail at once to see if Braysen is still there. And we shall increase our spy surveillance of both the Bizh and Hohdan empires." He mused for a *centisheg*. "Perhaps we should add one thing more—a hunch I have; we might send a light force down the arm to have another look at that Terran home world."

Gusten blinked. "I don't suppose you mean that a few might have survived there after all?"

"No. But there were machinery and materials left on that planet. Working quickly in suits, and being decontaminated afterward, someone—the survivors we are talking about, for instance—might reclaim useful things." He leaned forward in his chair. "We shall discuss this again soon. Meanwhile, I wish you to begin organizing a staff—closemouthed, practical individuals, sidestepping rank and protocol where it seems wise—to implement a real investigation. I feel that the seriousness of this affair warrants our stepping—discreetly, of course—outside the limits of our own responsibility."

(10)

THE HOHDAN unarmed dispatch ship dropped toward a green planet. John and Bart Lange sat before a large viewscreen in the lounge. John leaned forward and turned knobs to give a magnified view of a mountain range a few miles to one side. "If those aren't exactly like pines, I can't see the difference!"

Bart shrugged. "I'll wait until I can smell them before I get excited. Can you see the depot area yet?"

"No, but I think it's just off the corner of the screen, near that lake. There's a small strip of meadow bordering the lake, and the stuff's under the trees beyond the meadow. What do you think of the planet? Will you like calling it 'home'?"

Bart glanced at him. They were being prudent about what they said; conceivably, Vez Do Han, in the control room, might have listening devices planted in the lounge.

John grinned. He was excited, enough so Vez would notice it, if Vez were secretly listening and watching. But the attractive world below them wasn't the main cause of his excitement. As soon as he got clear of this world and of Vez, he had a rendezvous with the Omniarch.

The intercom grated, whistled, and said in Hohdan, "Planetfall in ten *dolek*." That would be about twenty-two minutes.

John and Bart started toward their quarters to get their luggage. The arrangement was that they'd stay here, just the two of them, and wait for *Luna,* which would be nulling in with a cargo of food from Akiel. Not that this planet wasn't bountiful, but there'd be no processing until a

73

plant was built, so an already packaged supply was to be laid in.

What John didn't know for sure was whether the Omniarch would be coming from Akiel with the ship or whether he'd merely send coordinates of some rendezvous point. John doubted very much that the ancient being would risk showing himself here. It didn't matter—things were moving.

In their quarters, a ping sounded, and a screen lit up, showing Vez's face. "I'll meet you at Hatch Number Two as soon as we touch down. All right?"

"Fine."

The sun felt like Sol. The trees bordering this meadow were not the pinelike ones—they had crinkly oval leaves, and the smell was like pepperwood—but they made John's pulse move faster. The grass, to casual examination, was Earth grass, ankle-deep in the lushest spots, and it *smelled* like grass.

The commonest type of birds might have been jays except for their purplish feathers instead of the sharply, painfully remembered blue. Filling the ecological niche of squirrels was a creature that, at first sight, looked startlingly like a very small Mexican hairless dog but which scuttled up, down, and around tree trunks as no dog of any sort ever did. Then there was a raccoonlike animal they got a glimpse of, ambling sleepily from the woods toward the lake, before it saw them, stared for a moment, shot an incredulous glance at the ship parked domineeringly a hundred yards away, and whirled to gallop back into cover with a sound that was almost a human gasp. John thought of it as raccoonlike mainly because of the way it moved. Actually it had a longer snout, like an opossum's, a short tail, and a pelt of dapple gray with only one spot of white on it, at the chest.

Vez, standing beside John and Bart (with armed Hohdan crewmen a few yards away, in case some dangerous animal should come charging out of the woods), smiled. "Do you like it, friends and comrades-in-arms?"

John had to swallow before he could speak. "It's . . . perfect, Vez. This is just how Earth, in its temperate latitudes and at this height above sea level, would feel in late spring."

Vez made a hand gesture. "I am glad. I ordered my ecologists to study your description of Earth before we chose. I am assured—though, you understand, the exploration was brief—that you can camp at any place near this lake, with only ordinary precautions against inimical native animals. Are you sure a tent will be adequate? We could quickly erect a bungalow. . . ."

John said, "The tent will be fine—less conspicuous."

Vez made the fist-open gesture. "I understand, though I have not looked at it myself, that there is a plateau a few miles downstream where you can build a village and all the simple production facilities you'll need. I'm contemplating that, should you acquire any considerable number of ships, you will work out methods of camouflage. So far as this temporary depot is concerned, no doubt you will find it convenient to land only two or three ships here at a time. And since the ground here is not firm enough to support mechanical derricks, you will find it necessary to use grav slings for onloading munitions."

They were walking toward the munitions dump. It occupied the lower fifty yards of the strip of woods adjoining the meadow. Over the big crates and cannisters was netting hung with strips of cloth (properly pigmented, Vez assured them, to match the foliage by any light—visible, infrared, or ultraviolet).

What a mountain of destruction slumbered under those nets! John's pulse stirred at the thought of the long missiles streaking out in salvo to pursue frantically dodging ships. *What a mess I am*, he thought. *Thrilled one minute by the smell of grass, the next by the thought of unleashing hell.*

Better, he told himself, that he forgo *all* feeling—and get on with the job he and his handful of men had to do.

The big ship *Luna* settled gingerly onto the meadow.

She'd hover just an inch above the grass, so as not to leave marks.

Coulter was first to emerge from the hatch. John met him. "Did you bring a passenger?"

"No. Just a set of coordinates and a time."

"Where and when?"

"About twelve and a half light-years from here, between four stars of a double binary so we'll be damned well camouflaged from mass detectors. Anytime later than"—Coulter looked at his wrist chronometer—"eleven hours from now."

John made a face. "Doesn't leave much time to offload your cargo and rearm the ship."

Coulter said, "We aren't to take *Luna* anyway. We're to go back to Akiel and take one of the small ships. It seems as if there's too close a watch on this big tub, or might be. The Full Male on Akiel suggested that Vez Do Han might already be suspicious. . . ."

John sighed. "He's probably right. Well, it means only an extra two hours. Were there any other instructions?"

"Yes, there should be about a dozen of us, plus somebody to take the small ship back to Akiel again. Or to here, if you're willing."

"I am; there ought to be someone here anyway to keep an eye on things. We'll be sending the Armed Scouts here two at a time to load missiles and fuel wire. Well, let's get on with the unloading. I guess we'll just pile the supplies under the trees."

(11)

WITH A NERVOUSNESS he tried not to show, John watched the Omniarch program for null. This was going to be a hop of several light-years—direct to the target planet, with no zeroing-in hop. Such a trip, unless you had very exact coordinates, was called "null roulette." But maybe the Omniarch knew what he was doing.

The small ship's mass-detector globe showed two big blips fairly close—one pair of binaries—and two others farther from the globe's center, that pair representing the other binaries. This was a good clandestine meeting place.

The big Chelki swiveled his head to look at John. "Ten seconds, Commodore."

John tried to relax.

Null!

Objective elapsed time was less than a minute and a half, but that was plenty long! A ship emerging from null could kick aside a fist-sized chunk of rock, but not much more. He perspired, swallowed hard, wishing he had a *muzhee* of *dron* or at least a good strong slug of whiskey. He clenched and unclenched his sweating fingers. The chronometer second hand stuttered toward the mark. He tried hard not to cringe. . . .

Breakout!

And they were still alive—and practically in orbit around a planet that might have been Mars except that this world had only a few visible craters. He glanced at instruments. An atmosphere . . . not over ten pounds per square inch . . . Some oxygen. He looked at another viewscreen. The planet's sun was a puny, fading dwarf that must have burned all life off the planet in its, the sun's, hot heyday.

And the planet *was* barren, though small seas remained.

They were well within the Hohdan region, furtively, and John's excitement about the Klee ship that was promised didn't offset his discontent. He didn't like playing under-handed with Vez Do Han.

But here they were. . . .

The Omniarch's big furry hands moved casually over the keyboard. The ship dropped. Air began to whistle around the hull. They moved laterally and came to a hover above one end of an oblong mesa. The Omniarch turned his head again. "There is minor excavation to do before the major one, John Braysen. I suggest the gentle applica-tion of a rupter beam to break up soil into dust, then a compressed-air nozzle to blow it away."

John, happy enough just to be alive after that null hop, shrugged. "You're the doctor. Where do you want to dig?"

"Not to dig, really. At a spot in the lee of this end of the mesa below us there is a metal object, two feet in diameter and a foot thick, about twenty feet below the surface. We can pinpoint it with a magnetometer."

John said, "All right, if you don't call twenty feet dig-ging. What's down there—a turret or something project-ing from the Klee ship?"

"No, John Braysen—it is no part of the ship itself. It is a remote-control device that will bring the ship to us—and that would baffle anyone who found it, not having gnawed away as I have at the few bits of Klee technology known to present cultures. Let us land and locate the device and get to work quickly."

They located the thing and got it uncovered without much difficulty. It looked like a large metal hatbox with no visible way of getting it open. Rapped with the knuckles, the metal sounded and felt thick and solid, but the thing was obviously hollow (unless it was an impossibly light metal).

The first peculiarity was the way of getting it open.

The Omniarch, who had made sure the small ship's supplies included magnet wire and a length of flexible plastic hose, proceeded to wind an unfamiliar but simple kind of coil. He wound the magnet wire in a helix (a very long one) around the hose. Then he coiled the helix into a toroid of three and a fraction turns, which fit snugly around the ancient control device. He fixed it in place with many wrappings of strong tape.

"Now," he told John, "we must have a pulsating direct current—a few amperes will do—the frequency of which we can vary between, let us say, five hundred and fifteen hundred megacycles per second. Does this ship have anything of the sort?"

John stared at the four-legged being incredulously. To come all this way . . . Then he saw something like humor in the nonhumanoid face, and suddenly flushed. "Of course. We just disconnect leads from the rupter—if you don't need more power than a couple of hundred watts—" Which was all this Armed Scout's small rupter used.

The Omniarch smiled. "It would have been indiscreet to bring special apparatus." He paused and breathed deeply, shifting his feet about a little. "Forgive me if I appear a little excited. I have seen only movies—I think that is your word—of the ship we'll be bringing here unless something fails. And it represents an important step in my plans, as well as a big increment of Klee technology."

Again John stared. "You mean *you've never used this remote-control device before?*"

"Oh, yes, I have used *that,* with very exciting results. In fact, I buried it here, several of your life spans ago. But the ship itself . . . Well, you shall see!"

A few minutes later current was running through the makeshift coil. The Omniarch stood over the device, legs spread wide, neck bent to the side to let him peer down. In his hands he held a small instrument—the dismounted frequency selector of the rupter weapon. He turned a knob slowly. Nothing seemed to be happening.

Then, suddenly, the ancient device shivered, shook, leaped a few inches into the air, and shed its top surface

like the lid of a hatbox popping off! Only the wrappings of
tape kept it loosely in place.

The Omniarch began, with unsteady hands, to remove
the tape and coil. And when those, and the lid of the
device, were off, John stared at an intricate mass of com-
ponents, dials, and markings. He recognized the Klee
script—though no one had ever made any headway deci-
phering it.

The big Chelki's hands were even shakier as he knelt,
one leg at a time, on the ground beside the device and
reached down to touch knobs. He drew a deep breath and
looked up at John. "If I understood the movie correctly,
and what little I have been able to decipher of various
directions—and if the Klee technology is as infallible as I
have reason to believe—the ship will break out of the
ground less than a mile from here. Perhaps we had best
get in your ship and go aloft. This planet's volcanic activity
is long since dead, but the power I am about to tap is
colossal, and there might be a small spillover."

Dazed, pulse pounding in his temples, John hurried into
the ship after the Omniarch, who carried the control
device. John punched at the ship's keyboard. And from an
altitude of five thousand feet—and ten miles to one side—
John watched and listened with the ship's sensors as the
Chelki adjusted, then hesitantly activated the device.

For a few minutes nothing happened, and he began to
tremble with angry disappointment. Then something did
happen. And his immediate panicky impulse, which he
managed to suppress, was to jab frantically at the keyboard and send them leaping skyward under seventeen
gees of acceleration.

First the planet's surface, the reddish bare crusted desert a mile beyond the mesa, split. It heaved up, not in a
spot, but along a line. The split and upheaval spread to the
sides and became a huge plot of dirt and dust and rocks—
and, after a minute or two, mud—rising and tumbling
aside, as if a gigantic submarine were disinterring itself
out of solid ground.

The noise reached the ship—a roar. Not an explosion, but simply the cascade of dirt and shattered rock tumbling to the sides. And, too, perhaps, the actual sound of the rock being shattered. For whatever was coming up was coming up from deep down.

A cloud of dust partly obscured the area, so that at first he couldn't see what *was* coming up. Then, on a level keel, serenely, slowly, majestically—as if those millions of tons of rock were a few motes of dust—the ship rose into the air.

He sat paralyzed, unbelieving, too stunned to look at dials that might have told him his eyes were not lying.

Four thousand feet long, if it was a foot! Six or seven hundred feet in diameter! Cylindrical except that it had curved ends—not hemispherical ones, but rather with a paraboloidal shape. Like the smaller end of a hen's egg.

How ludicrous even to *think* of anything "small," while looking at this immensity!

There were no turrets or protuberances visible from this distance (though some fairly big ones would, of course, be too small to see from here). There were bands or markings around the ship at intervals—chainlike markings—no! Series of circular spots, not touching one another, but each series forming one of the "bands." There were—somehow his mind stirred itself to count—eighteen of the "bands," and each must consist of forty or fifty circles if they extended clear around the ship.

Then he saw the thing in another mental perspective and realized that those circles (round spots, actually) were probably hatch covers, of a darker metal or painted darker than the dull-silver of the continuous area of the hull.

Hundreds of hatches. Each, if it were open, big enough to admit the ship he was in now.

Suddenly he realized that the monster was still rising and was almost level with them. He whirled toward the Omniarch. "Hey! Can't you—"

But the Chelki was already turning knobs in the remote-control gadget. John shot a glance at the viewscreen.

The incredible ship had stopped rising and now hovered even with them. He saw one of the hatches slide (no, almost jerk) open.

The Omniarch was smiling his thin-lipped smile, though his eyes were almost wild with excitement. "Shall we board your new ship, Commodore John Braysen?"

The real necessity for having a crew of a dozen men lay not in operating grav and null drives, hatches, or internal machinery—the controls for those were fairly easy to identify in the big midship Main Control Room—but in learning more about the ship.

They were back at the Omniarch's rendezvous among the stars of the double binary. By cautious testing of various switches, studs, and keyboards, they'd already traced out the immense ship's internal communications system, so that men in various parts of the ship could report to Main Control what was happening. And baffling things did happen in response to various switches in the Control Room (or in response to corresponding switches in the auxiliary control rooms near either end of the ship). Massive mountings in big weapons bays swiveled, without giving any hints as to what kind of weapons had once been mounted. Telltale lights of half a dozen colors winked in compartments where power leads were carefully blocked off with plastic insulation. Klaxons sounded at unexpected times, warning of nothing discernible except that certain studs in a control room had been pressed. And huge, sealed, thick-walled columns hummed with power amounting to millions of kilowatts—to no discernible purpose!

John and the Omniarch did not, of course, stroll about flipping switches at random. Before they even dared turn on a light, they had spent many hours confirming (as well as possible) what the Omniarch already suspected—that the ship possessed such an array of automatic safeguards that even the most reckless imbecile could not make it harm itself. And of course, they could already recognize warnings, on various bits of equipment, in the ancient script. The Omniarch had already deciphered the script and language to that extent.

Also, there was another thing that puzzled John at first. "This," he said, frowning over the third or fourth clear warning inscription, "is too damned much of a coincidence. My own world used the color red to mean danger. So do the Hohdans, and so do the Vulmoti. And apparently the Klee did too!"

The Omniarch smiled. "No coincidence, John Braysen. My own species did too, when we had a culture of our own. Think—do we not all have red blood? And is not the symbolism very clear?"

John looked at him quickly, flushed a little, and grinned. "You're right. We'd be in a hell of a fix, wouldn't we, if we found artifacts of some species with green blood?"

"I suspect," the Omniarch said, "that we'd learn quickly, the hard way."

It was obvious that the Klee had used virtually all the technologies currently in existence—and in addition a number of totally strange ones.

For example, in the Main Control Room there was one panel to the side of the biggest console that was mounted on what seemed to be springs. The springs, at all four corners, were of some unfamiliar plastic or ceramic, very tough and hard, and so rigid that John couldn't squeeze two adjacent coils even slightly together with all the strength of his fingers. Instrument dials on the panel totaled sixty-seven—mostly in rows of three, each trio obviously representing the same thing but in some sort of vernier system. But there were a few single dials, and some sets of two.

There was a large number of switches, studs, and knobs. The Omniarch, pausing before he left the room, smiled and answered John's query cryptically: "Experiment with it a bit. Nothing you can do on this panel is dangerous."

John looked after him for a moment, then, a little piqued, turned to stare at the panel. It was about six feet high and ten feet long, set eight or nine inches out from the plane of the console, with sides, inset a little from the springs, that almost touched the console, so that the space behind the panel was hidden. No doubt there were instruments and wiring there.

All the switches were off. He chose one below the biggest feature of the panel—a dark but slightly translucent disk more than three feet in diameter near one end. He flipped the switch to "On"—and dodged back as a transparent sphere, the diameter of the disk, seemed to materialize instantly!

He approached it cautiously. There was no light in it, but light from the room penetrated. The dark disk was gone. Half of the sphere bulged out from where it had been. The other was beyond it—beyond the panel—as if there were at least a foot and a half of space there. He put out a finger to touch the surface.

And felt nothing. His finger simply penetrated what looked like a glass or plastic sphere. He jerked it back— and the sphere was still there, unmarked. An uneasy sensation rippled up his spine. He turned the switch off, and the sphere vanished. The darkly translucent disk was back again. He once more flipped the switch, and the sphere returned.

An optical phenomenon of some kind, then! He stared at it for a minute, then suddenly turned and hurried over to the mass-detector apparatus. Yes, the transparent sphere there—in which points of light showed, representing the four stars of the double binary, with tinier blips which represented his Armed Scout and *Luna* (now here)—was the same size! He reached very cautiously across the railing that surrounded it, and touched the surface.

This sphere was what it looked like—solid, cool to the touch. He went back to the spring-mounted panel.

None of the other switches brought any blips to life in the illusionary sphere, nor could he get so much as a flicker out of dial needles. He frowned over inscriptions. Only one word did he recognize, in the largest script—actually the title for the whole panel, running down one side. The word meant "null," or so the Omniarch translated it.

Well, this was some special kind of mass detector, no doubt, that could be activated only when the computers were programmed to null. Maybe it showed the building-up null charges of nearby ships, or something like that. He turned off the switch.

Equally puzzling was the arrangement of four chronometers above a small auxiliary-computer keyboard. When the master switch of that keyboard was closed, the four clocks immediately began running—but there was an instant of quick cycling, hands spinning at varying rates, until the four took up what appeared to be four separate times. Each of three showed dates and times, in Klee script, that John couldn't understand at all. The fourth ran at the same rate as his wrist chronometer (though of course the numerals and calibration were entirely different).

And, if things in sight were mysterious, hidden things were more so! The core of the ship, a huge sealed unit over a thousand feet long and close to two hundred feet in diameter, was not only inaccessible, but seemed never to have had any means of access! So solid, so thick to sonar and magnetic sounding, so massively moored into the ship was that core, that John and the Omniarch agreed upon its having been cast in some gigantic mold, and the ship built around it. Or possibly it had been assembled of various pieces, then had a jacket of continuous metal somehow plated around it. That plating (if it *were* a plating) was of the same metal as the hull, far harder and more resistant than any steel.

But, though the core's wall thickness must be twenty feet or more, it was hollow inside, and the ship's main machinery, such as the energy converters, was somewhere inside. Great conduits came out, bearing wattages that would have melted the heaviest conduits of any other ship John had ever seen. So the converters *must* be in there. He grumbled to himself about it for twenty hours or so before talking to the Omniarch. "There must be a hell of a supply of fuel in there! No way to replace it, if it's ever used up. Do you think the Klee build ships like this on a disposable basis? Stock them with fuel, and when it's used up, just throw the ship away? Or would they take some kind of a cutting torch and *make* a way in?"

The Omniarch smiled. "As you say, there could be a hell of a supply in that core."

John looked at him for a minute. The Chelki was being too secretive to suit him. "By the way, you've never told me how you got that remote-control device. Nor where you saw movies that taught you where this ship was hidden and a few things about its operation. And—it occurs to me that there may have been directions for finding other Klee artifacts. Militarily useful ones, I mean."

The Omniarch blinked twice in affirmation. "Do you think I have not searched, John Braysen? Other items may have been destroyed in natural catastrophes. Or they may still be waiting. Please realize, John Braysen, that I am not free to move about entirely as I wish. The Vulmoti have spies in many places."

John didn't reply. But he thought he'd gained a little information—presumptive information, anyway. The place where the Omniarch had found the control device and seen the movie (God knew what it was printed on, to have lasted so long) was probably somewhere in the Vulmot region. The Omniarch used that word "place" when he wanted to avoid giving any hints.

He'd also said the live women were in a "place."

After a hundred hours (during the last eighty of which Bart Lange had been aboard) John was sure he could operate the vast ship without the Omniarch. The grav drives and the null apparatus were simple enough. He did have to program corresponding English equivalents for Klee terminology into the computers, but enough of that was done by now to get by on, and more could be added gradually. The matter of Klee mathematics was simpler; after all, computers could as easily translate Arabic numerals and a decimal system as the duodecimal-based Klee arithmetic. At first he'd intended to recalibrate all the instrument dials, painting on English words and Arabic numerals, but he soon realized that it would be easier simply to learn to interpret the dials as they were.

The Omniarch departed, taking the remote-control device with him. John didn't like that but didn't protest.

Most of his men arrived, a shipload at a time. The Armed Scouts all came aboard, to be hidden in the big bays. Living quarters were set up, and galleries, and recreation halls. And now John turned his thoughts to armament, leaving Bart Lange in charge of further studying the controls and instrumentation.

That immense hull, the mere fact of its existence, implied and actually proved the tremendous strength of the metal. There were stocks of the stuff, in huge panels, in a storage hold; and Bart was going to have bits sawed off and test them for physical and chemical properties. But the hatch covers, those great disks arranged in eighteen bands, like tight-fitting necklaces around the ship, were of steel only. A splendid kind of steel—perhaps the ultimate in possible iron alloys—but still steel, much weaker and susceptible to corrosion and impact than the metal of the hull and of structural members inside. That would be a liability in combat, of course.

It occurred to him to wonder why—the ship being so ancient—that steel wasn't already rusted away. Maybe it had been protected, in its great underground chamber, by utter dryness of the air (and why air?) or by some chemical means.

But there was one advantage in those hatch covers of lesser metal: they could be torch-cut, and welded onto, much more readily. And to install orthodox weapons (missile launchers, laser clusters, rupters) in the great bays, he'd have to cut ports in the big hatch covers. So that was all right.

He pondered that question of installation. There were engineers among his men, of course, and a gunnery officer who could plan the mounting and wiring. But the volume of work would be tremendous.

Would the Omniarch let it be done on Akiel? No, surely not. All the work would have to be done in space, by human hands. Well, work was only work.

`And that left one other question: where to get the weapons? He decided to talk over his idea about that with Bart Lange.

"We had some chance," he said, "of capturing Bizh ships in salvageable condition when we started the raids. That chance is gone now. They're too thoroughly alerted. And we can't ask Hohd for more weapons—they'd prick up their ears like foxes. And we can't buy them anywhere, even a few at a time, because we have nothing to pay for them with."

Bart shrugged agreement and waited for him to continue.

John said, "I've been thinking that the Vuls probably never bothered to salvage much, if anything, from Earth. There was a tremendous production going on, that just stopped dead at the Destruction." *Dead indeed,* he thought. "There was a lot of stuff they could have used—but it would have been a real project to go down and salvage it, working in suits, and decontaminate it."

Bart sat up straighter. "You don't think, do you, that just lying around for eight years has cleaned it up to any extent?"

"To some extent, surely. Not enough; but by working in shifts, well suited up, we could get cargoes off-planet. Rain will have washed a lot of the dirtiest stuff out of the atmosphere. And munitions lying in warehouses and factories won't have been badly contaminated, anyway. Once in space, we can decontaminate things—including men in suits." He watched Bart's face. "Say we pick up a hundred missile launchers, and fifty laser clusters, and fifty heavy rupters. . . ."

Bart squirmed forward in his chair. "I imagine the lasers were probably ruined immediately."

"Maybe so; we can find out. But if we haul everything to some place with no atmosphere, and wash it down repeatedly with lots of water containing boron compounds or something . . ."

Bart grinned. "What would we haul it in? You're talking about a big load, and a lot of radioactivity."

"True—but we've got a *big* ship. We can sacrifice a thousand feet of it, if need be." He smiled at Bart's expression. "I don't mean chop it off—I'd hate to try to cut around this hull, anyway—I mean, just stow the stuff in one end, and cut off air circulation from that end, and only enter it in suits to do the work. Later, we might be able to sweep out that end well enough. If we can't—so what? There aren't enough of us to fill a thousandth of the ship anyway!"

Bart jumped to his feet. "Damn! It's worth a try! And I'll bet there are a lot of things we never heard of that'll speed up decontamination!"

John told him, "I fully intend to blackmail the Omniarch for any knowledge he or his technician-gender descendants have along those lines. But even at worst, what if a missile launcher *did* give off a few R's? Once it's installed, we can stay away from it most of the time. In this ship, we can detour a good comfortable way around things."

"We damned well can," Bart agreed abstractedly. He was excited now, and thinking hard. "How much of a crew will we take?"

"More," John told him, "than we can rustle up suits for. There'll be a lot of work to do. In fact, I thought we'd take nearly everybody, except for skeleton crews aboard *Luna* and a couple of the smaller ships. Morale's been sagging a little lately. A look at Earth might bolster it. Most of the men never saw her, after . . ."

Bart pondered, then nodded slowly. "I think you're right. For that matter, I don't think I could resist the chance, now. It's a ghoulish thing, maybe, but . . . Well, I want to see how she looks after being dead for eight years."

THE ANCIENT, immense ship had been in null for almost four hours—nearly enough for the trip to Sol. John restlessly paced the big Control Room. Instincts were nagging at him.

After eight years, unless there were some immediate stimulus, there should be no logical reason for the Vuls to be maintaining a watch on the Solar System. True, mining operations could be carried out in the presence of lingering radioactivity, but why should a rich, powerful empire bother? Anything that could be found on, in, or around Sol's planets could be found on thousands of planetary bodies *without* radioactivity. And, so far as Earth's stocks of completed and semicompleted weapons were concerned —well, these wouldn't interest Vulmot for a similar reason: it would be easier to manufacture the same items elsewhere than to reclaim and decontaminate anything from Earth. John's only reason for undertaking that labor was that he had no other place to get the things.

But still, he was nervous. After all, he might have already given the Vuls reason to think again of Earth. If they were astute enough, or lucky enough, to guess that men were involved in the hit-and-run attacks against forward outposts of the Bizh Empire, they might follow the same chain of logic he had.

He glanced at a chronometer. Less than a quarter-hour now to the planned breakout—no farther from the sun than Pluto, but, to avoid planetoids, well outside the plane of the ecliptic.

If the Vuls *had* set up a watch on the Solar System,

they'd undoubtedly be aground on planets or planetoids, safely camouflaged from mass detectors. And they'd be already charged for null, while this big ship would *not* be. He and Bart had established that her time for recharging was faster than that of ordinary ships (three minutes and twenty seconds instead of four minutes), but that was still a long time, in terms of space combat.

He could not be sure that the great hull of unknown metal could resist the armaments of capital ships or even heavy cruisers.

He went to stand beside the mass-detector sphere at one end of the big console. Bart came to stand at his elbow. "I wish," Bart said, "we had this thing calibrated better. When we break out, it'll be full of blips—Sol and the planets—but I don't know whether any of the planetoids and satellites will show. And if it happens that we have to run, I'd like to know exactly where we are!"

John nodded. All the blips should lie in a plane four or five inches below the center of the sphere, which of course represented the ship's position. Sol would show as a green-blue intense blip, but the rest of the system might be confused—especially as, after more than eight years, he didn't have an accurate plot of the planets' positions in orbit. He started another turn about the room.

And suddenly he had a hunch. He stopped and looked fixedly at the spring-mounted panel with the weirdly incomprehensible illusionary sphere. The script on that panel said something about null. . . .

He strode to the thing and flipped on the switch below the semitranslucent dark disk. The optical illusion of a sphere leaped into apparent being—and it was cluttered with multicolored blips of light!

He gaped for a few moments. "Bart! Come here!"

Bart Lange came, running the last few steps. Then he stopped and stared. "But—what the hell! We're in *null!*"

John was grinning now and shaking with excitement. "We are that. And this thing *sees* from null! Look—that's got to be Sol; and those are the planets. Green! Cute, eh? Green for planets? Blue-green for the star. And—Bart—

look—every one of those amber blips is the same distance from a green blip! Five or six millimeters." He stared at the arrangement for a minute. "Some of those green blips are planetoids, though. I guess the gadget doesn't differentiate."

Suddenly he looked up at Bart. *"Do you know what I think those amber blips are?"*

Bart Lange blinked at him for a moment, then gasped. He drew a deep breath. "I think I do, John. Those are—are ships, alive and powered. A task force—thirty ships or more—all on the surface of some planet or big asteroid. Now, don't ask me if I know how this wizard ship can register an enemy fleet—at this distance, *and from null*. I won't even listen to that question!" Suddenly he grinned. "I'll bet you ten feet of fuel wire to one that there are other tricks in this gadget." He leaned forward, selected a knob, and turned it slowly. The pattern of blips in the nonmaterial sphere shrank toward the center, without altering relative positions. The knob stopped turning. "That," Bart chuckled, "is the setting for extreme range." He turned the knob the other way. It kept turning in this direction—clockwise—until the pattern of blips had expanded to more than the diameter of the sphere. "There goes Pluto. There goes Uranus, and Neptune!"

The knob reached its other extreme. By then the whole Solar System had vanished—range had been reduced too much as the scale increased. Bart pointed to a small white blip. "What do you suppose that is? A wandering chunk of rock?"

John shrugged. "I'd guess, a comet—frozen gases, or ice. The Klee went in for symbolism, obviously."

"Yes." Bart made a face. "'You know—this isn't going to be all peaches and cream! We'll be able to see any chunk of debris within a hundred light-years. It won't be comfortable, knowing how much junk we might null right through."

John told him, "On the contrary—if we ever find ourselves about to break out inside something, we can avoid it. This practically eliminates zeroing in!"

Bart looked startled, then grinned sheepishly. "I guess that's right. Say, why didn't we discover this—this magician's gadget before? We've been in null with this ship a dozen times!"

John tried to recall each hop, and precisely what they'd done in the way of experimentation. "I guess we simply didn't have this panel activated when we were near enough to anything to see it." He looked up at the dials above the illusionary sphere. "There's a lot of data being shown right now. Will you add this to your studies?"

"What do *you* think?" He turned and looked at the breakout chronometer. "Are we going on in as far as we intended?"

John had already made that decision. "No. We're going to stop out of mass-detector range—which will be quite a distance, with this big lummox. Then we're going to pinpoint Earth's position very exactly and null practically into atmosphere. Unless, of course, we find an amber blip alongside Earth."

Bart said, "There wasn't one. They were scattered around the system farther out. Of course, they could move, but I'm betting they won't. This has the smell of an ambush."

John nodded. "And we might still fall into it. I expect they make a pass over Earth now and then, just in case something has sneaked by them." He turned and walked toward his seat. He turned on the shipwide intercom. "All hands stand by for breakout. And, incidentally—battle stations aboard all Armed Scouts! It seems there are visitors in the Solar System. We're going to try to dodge them, but if it happens that they see us and come running to stare at an impossibly big ship, we just might spit you out like a bunch of aroused hornets. If we do, hit them hard until you can null. I'm going to program battle plans and a null rendezvous right now."

He was aware of Bart grinning and muttering and shaking his head dazedly.

The great ship hung over what had once been eastern

Sumatra. Wherever they could, men sat or stood silently
staring at viewscreens. John (who'd seen Earth, as most of
the others had not, in her early death) was as shaken as
anybody.

Somehow he'd expected a bare planet by now: rocks
broiling in the sun, brown soil scored into corduroy by
unhindered rain. When he'd been here, leaves still hung
from trees—brown and shriveled, but mostly not yet fall-
en. He expected to see all that gone.

But Earth had not been favored with even a decent
burial.

The trees, most of them, still stood. A few miles to one
side of the ship, a blackened area marked the passage of a
forest fire, but even there blackened stumps thrust accus-
ingly toward the sky. And even some of the *leaves* had not
fallen. What remained hung in a shriveled travesty of life.
There'd been very little decay, of course—decay was a
form of life, and it had stopped along with the rest when
the radioactivity began to seep through bark and heart-
wood. And roots were still intact, to a considerable extent
holding together the dead soil against the erosion even of
this heavy-rainfall area. Oh, there was bare earth, especially in the burned-over region, but in most places some
sort of litter still existed.

And the wooden buildings were even more eerie. Was it
not a kind of blasphemy that weathered boards, in this wet
climate, should show no fungus rot? No termite action, no
gnawed ratholes? And, under a peak of eaves, should a
bird's nest of twigs still cling, with eggs still waiting there as
if they needed only the love of a feathered breast to hatch
them?

There were, of course, carcasses and corpses. Withered
bodies of men and women and children and water buffalo
lay about, the humans mostly curled into balls, the beasts
with their heads outstretched, their limbs stiffly straight.
John saw one dog huddled beside the corpse of a young
boy. Which had died first? Which had crawled to the other
for whatever comfort of spirit, if not body, company
might offer?

He began to hear mutterings from the intercom as sickness and rage broke the silent staring of the men.

To the west loomed mountains, the highest peaks bare and rocky. The glimmer of a lake showed in the foothills as the immense ship lifted to cross the summit. It was odd, somehow, to see a lake—John tended, he mused, to feel subconsciously that a lake was a living thing. And what of the seacoast the ship was about to cross? Wasn't it wrong for the surf to crawl and bunch up and boom with life?

He bent forward to flip a switch. "Doctor?"

"Yes, sir."

"How soon will you have a report on the atmosphere?"

"Another hour for a complete report, Commodore. But I can say right now that there's still enough Strontium 90 to be deadly. And traces of Cobalt 60—that's surprising, isn't it? You don't think of cobalt as a metal that can be divided into small enough particles to stay in the atmosphere very long. Probably there's enough picked up by the wind from somewhere to be detectable."

John frowned. "Cobalt 60? How would that happen?"

The physicist grunted. "Maybe a warhead made a direct hit on a warehouse where ordinary cobalt metal was stored. That's all it would take, I think."

"I suppose so." John pondered for a moment. "How about things in general? Would you say there's enough residual radioactivity, in the ground and in buildings and whatnot, to get through to a man in a suit?"

"I'm afraid so, if he stayed around very long and touched too many things. Maybe with special mittens that had layers of absorptive compounds . . ."

"We have those," John told him. "What about just walking around in the open air? Would too much get through the suit?"

"I think not, unless he walked around in the rain. I can only guess about that."

John sighed. "All right. Thanks." He got slowly from his seat and walked over to Bart Lange. "I think we'll try the Balkans first. There was a lot of heavy production there just before the Destruction. And it's a dry season there right now." He eyed Bart for a minute. "I'm leaving you in command aboard."

Lange stared, then scowled. "You don't mean *you* are going aground, do you? That's ridiculous! You're not expendable!"

John felt a rush of annoyance. "Damn it, do you think I can keep the respect of the men if I stay aboard and send them down into that? It's no ordinary thing down there, Bart, that a man's instincts can cope with, such as a tiger or a pack of wolves. Radioactivity's too stealthy. You can't see it or feel it, but you know how deadly it is. It works on your mind, whether instruments tell you it's too weak to hurt you or not. And a man would get to thinking about his commander sitting safe in a sealed ship. Anyway, we'll be carrying detectors. If *any* of us begins to pick up too much, we'll come back aboard in a hurry."

Lange looked convinced but disgusted. "What if the Vuls show up? Do you expect me to go off and leave you?"

"I certainly do. Look—we have to play the Omniarch's game. If we lose any considerable number here, he'll be forced to guard the rest of you like babies. In other words, whether it's expedient for his damned plan or not, he'd have to consider you unexpendable breeding stock. So I'm as expendable here as anyone else. The respect of the men *isn't* expendable, if we're going to go on as a group. Besides, I have to be on the ground to make the decisions as to what we take and how we handle it. And you're the only one I can depend on to know enough about this ship and have the right judgment if things go wrong."

Lange muttered disgustedly, sat silent for a minute, and finally shrugged. "All right; you're the commodore. What do you intend to do about power for cranes and whatnot?"

"The first thing we'll do on the ground is look for power sources still operable. If we don't find any, we'll have to run power lines from the ship. We can do that without leaving any pathways for radioactivity to get aboard."

"I guess so. How long do you expect to stay down, the first shift?"

"Ten hours, including the time to suit up and the time to decontaminate us afterward and get us out of the suits. I can't ask men to work any longer, or even to stay in the suits under a planet's gravity, without rest or a decent meal. I'll take about twenty with me the first shift. If everything goes all right, a bigger crew can go down for the second shift. It's going to be a hectic time for everyone, aground or aboard, what with the job of decontamination and whatever else we run into. I don't expect we'll foresee all the problems."

Bart sighed. "Hell, no. When will you take the first shift down?"

"As soon as we've chosen the factories and have a look at them from the air. We'll start suiting up right after the next meal."

The suits, though they were made of the lightest materials possible, including plastics and magnesium-aluminum alloys, so their mass wouldn't be too high, were intended mainly for use in free fall, not on planets. Consequently, movement in them was slow and labored. A survey tour that would have taken a half-hour without encumbrance took two hours in the suits.

John didn't permit himself to keep glancing nervously at the radiation-monitoring instrument built into the left sleeve of his suit. Nevertheless, he was nervous enough to perspire profusely, and the suit had trouble keeping up with the moisture. He felt clammy all over and found it easy to imagine that part of the discomfort might be radiation coming through the suit.

But the air wasn't seriously radioactive in terms of short exposure, and everyone avoided touching anything solid until it was checked.

In terms of actual work, they did better than he expected: during the seventh and eighth hours they managed to hoist seventeen finished missile launchers aboard the huge ship, which hovered a few inches above the pavement of a yard, opened hatches at one end, and dropped power cables.

A standard launcher was big—sixty feet long and almost nine in diameter, weighing over five tons—but fairly simple in principle and construction. It used a type of grav drive. There were shield plates at the butt end, solidly fixed to take an impact of a missile being loaded in, and activating coils embedded in casting metaloplast that could have withstood the impact of machine-gun bullets without cracking or distorting. Along the interior of the tube were smaller plates (a total of forty-eight) that, controlled by a surprisingly simple type of automatic computer, could vary their shielding to compensate for any natural gravity that existed or any inertial movement of the launcher. A missile remained exactly aligned along the axis of the tube.

The beauty of this standard launcher was that you could put *any* missile into it, up to a diameter of seven and a half feet, keep it aligned, and fire it with an unaugmented velocity of up to three thousand feet per second. There were also, of course, electrical connections so that a ship's fire-power computers could program into the missile whatever was called for—homing-on-heat, homing-on-mass, optical pursuit, prepatterned course, or games-theory erratic flight. Of course a launcher could be used also to propel simple torpedoes with no drives of their own, if velocity of three thousand feet per second were enough. You could even stick a plain bullet-shaped mass of metal (or any other matter) into the tube and fire it. Or even a very small boat or a life pod could be projected into space.

The practice of being shot, merely in a suit, at another ship—a cadet fad—was frowned upon. But a launcher was a very versatile piece of equipment.

There'd be considerable work installing these Earth-built launchers in the vast ancient ship. Their mountings wouldn't fit the launcher's trunnions. Even the threading on bolts and machine screws would have to be adapted. Electrical connectors would have to be changed. All that, though, offered no problems other than hard work and lots of it.

John was still pondering what he'd do for weapons ports. Those hatch covers of steel, when they opened, exposed a hole eighty-seven feet in diameter, more than enough for an Armed Scout or for various classes of dispatched ships to enter—and also more than enough to admit hostile missiles and energy beams. What he wanted was ports of about twenty feet in diameter, enough to give a launcher a moderate angle of fire. That, though, was simply another detail. For now he was happy just to have seventeen launchers in two big holds.

It was barely into the ninth hour when trouble came.

John had a crew inside the blocks-long warehouse, picking out more launchers the wheeled derrick could reach easily, when his suit earphones buzzed. "Braysen here," he said with a touch of foreboding.

The voice that came was Bart Lange's, and it was grim. "John—some Vul ships are headed toward Earth!"

John's midriff tightened. "Do you have them on mass detector already?"

"No. We've been doing a little playing around with instruments. You know those dials on the spring-mounted panel? Well, we noticed an identical set on the main console that we hadn't figured out a purpose for until now. There's a set of four switches—all of them have to be closed—that brings the same sort of detection system as that from null system onto these dials! And simultaneously the regular mass-detector sphere is cut in, so that you can see the amber blips and everything. And four ships are moving in from outer planets or asteroids. Since we're on the daylight side of Earth, we're hidden from them so far. But we won't be for long, if they come around—or even if they stop outside Earth's orbit. You were talking about a lot of lighting for the second shift down there."

John's pulse was pounding by now, and he suddenly felt very thirsty. He swallowed without relieving the feeling. "We'll have to cancel that. And listen—disconnect those power cables, close the hatches, and get aloft!"

There was a shocked pause. "You don't mean you want to *stay* down there!"

John was abruptly furious. "Damn it, Bart—listen!

We're in the middle of setting up things for the second shift. If we come aboard now, somebody'll have to start over later—and I won't be down here to make decisions. We're getting along fine on our suits' food tablets and water so far. There's no telling what those Vul ships intend to do; they might land somewhere to make a study, or they might orbit a few times, take pictures and instrument readings, and go away. But you can't sit there where you are; you'd be as conspicuous as a beetle on a white table-cloth. Get aloft into thin atmosphere so your null charge won't leak off—and be ready to hop."

Another pause. "John, are you crazy? Hop away and leave you, when we can just as well pick you up first?"

"It's *not* just as well, damn it! We're in the middle of a job down here. Go back out of their detector range and watch them. At the worst, you can null back again right over this spot and come down and pick us up. Move! You're wasting time!"

Now Bart was angry too. "All right, hero! How long do you want us to stay away?"

John hesitated. He'd made this decision without thinking —another one of his impulses. They ought to be able to stand a second ten hours in the suits. Radioactivity wasn't showing up as badly as they thought it might. . . . "Up to ten hours, depending on what the Vuls do. If you *have* to come down ready to fight—well, just remember that you can hit them with ten ships before they know what's happening. But don't do it unless you *have* to. Now move!"

Bart didn't reply. But within seconds the power cables dropped free of the big ship, the hatches slid shut, and she began to rise. John, standing in a warehouse door, watched her dwindle into the sky. He swallowed hard. Now that she was gone, he felt very tiny and very much alone—and foolish. Bart may have been right. . . .

Perhaps ten minutes passed. Then a heavy boom made his suit tremble—the vast implosion as the ship vanished in an instant from the upper atmosphere. He turned and looked into the gloom of the warehouse interior. The whole shift had heard his interchange with Bart Lange, and now most of them stood silently watching him. He couldn't see their eyes in the shade of their helmets. Guilt and doubt stabbed deeper into him. "Well," he said more gruffly than he intended, "let's get on with what we were doing, while the daylight lasts."

For a minute no one spoke, though two or three turned and started back to where they'd been working. Then someone—Fred Coulter—asked, "What are we going to do for power now that the ship's gone?"

John moved toward the warehouse door. "Find some. I'll drag those cables in out of sight. You, Fred, start lugging a bunch of those sealed-cell batteries we saw over here. The derrick'll take direct current, and we can put enough batteries in series to get the voltage."

None of them said any more just then. But their silence was expressive.

John felt giddy from the mugginess inside the suit and from the lack of solid food for thirteen hours. Also, in spite of the soaking humidity, and the water he sipped from the suit's still-adequate supply, he was thirsty. He knew that no amount of water was going to relieve that thirst, so he steeled himself to endure it. But it didn't help his feelings any.

If he only had a *muzhee* of *dron*. . . . He chuckled a little hysterically to himself. How would he get it into the suit, anyway? There was a miniature airlock in the chest, but he didn't want to let in deadly air, did he? Although if he opened it very carefully, put the pellet inside, and closed the outer lock . . . These suits were designed so that, by working at it, a man's left arm could be gotten out of the sleeve to use inside the suit.

He felt suddenly furious with himself. What was he maundering about? He didn't have any *dron* anyway.

He got to his feet, breath ragged, and walked around. *Anything* to relieve, if only by a trifle, that awful tingling restlessness of his muscles. . . . He wondered if the men felt as miserable as he did. One of them had been sobbing quietly a while back. The trapped feeling was maddening in itself, without the actual physical misery. . . . But none of them would be suffering from the thirst, the awful unquenchable thirst, the *dron* need. Unless Fred Coulter had picked up a little of it on Jessa.

He looked around. Where was Fred now? Oh, yes—over there against the wall, sitting with legs outsprawled, head bent as far forward as the suit allowed. If he were asleep, that was fine; fine. John wished he himself could sleep.

The sun must be almost down; the gloom was deep in the warehouse. No one was working anymore—they'd finished what they'd been doing, anyway, and John didn't trust himself to plan anything more. Most of them were sitting. A few were lying down.

He turned and ambled unsteadily to the doorway, started to put a gauntleted hand on the edge, then remembered—or thought he remembered—that this particular door jam was worse contaminated than some of the others. He peered out, looking for the man he'd posted on watch. "Cameron?" His voice was hoarse, blurred, cracked. "Cameron, where are you?" Then he saw the suited figure moving slowly along a building wall, at least fifty yards away. He felt a listless twinge of anger. Cameron should have stayed where he was posted. . . . John began to move tentatively in that direction, and Cameron, seeing him, lifted an unsteady hand to the suit's control studs at the left side of the chest. "Got his receiver turned off," John mumbled thickly. He puzzled about that for a minute. Was it a serious breach of orders or regulations?

What orders or regulations? The hell with them.

But then Cameron's voice was in John's earphones. "Do you want me, Commodore?"

It took John a minute to remember what he wanted to ask Cameron. "Did they . . . have you seen . . ."

Cameron, who seemed to be holding up very well, walked toward him. "They made another pass somewhere south of here a few minutes ago. Or was it a few hours? Anyway, I got a glimpse of it in the sunlight. And I could hear it through the suit's outside ears, so it must have been in atmosphere."

John sighed. Even sighing was an effort, he was so tired now. . . . He said, with no particular feeling, "I was worried when I didn't see you."

Cameron chuckled blurrily. "That was funny, Commodore—do you know why I went looking around over there? I guess I was half-asleep on my feet for a minute, and I went looking for a men's room."

John pondered that. He decided that it *was* funny. Sometime in the future, if there was a future, they might laugh about it. He stared into the darkening sky. He didn't trust his thinking right now, but he'd just about decided that the Vuls must have done some good thinking and sent a task force to the Solar System as a result. He drew a weary breath. "I don't see any need to keep a watch anymore, Jim. If you want to lie down someplace . . ."

James Cameron's face was barely visible in the fogged-up helmet, in this twilight, but he seemed to be looking at John. "I thought I'd stay out here anyway, Commodore. In case . . ."

"In case," John finished for him, "Bart Lange stretches his orders a little—they *were* vague—and comes back early. I was intending to stay out here too. They, I mean the Vuls, won't be able to see us or photograph us in this light. Let's sit down against the wall of the warehouse."

They didn't talk much. Once or twice—he didn't remember which—John hauled himself to his feet and trudged back inside to see how the men were doing. They were all sitting or lying down now. No one said anything. They were just—enduring.

He went back outside and sat down, though the sky was too dark to have shown the big ship unless it nulled to quite a ways out of atmosphere, and out of Earth's shadow. He stared at the chronometer in the left arm of the suit but couldn't make out the luminous figures. He feared that there were still at least five hours to wait. And then Bart might have to come down fighting, and in a fight close over a spot on a planet, things could happen. . . . John hardly cared right now. A bomb or an energy beam would be a mercy.

He told himself blurrily, you'll either survive, or you won't. And it's your fault that you're here in this fix. And stop sipping water—it only makes the bladder problem worse, and it won't relieve the thirst. And you're not going to get any *dron*.

He was asleep when Bart Lange's voice suddenly blared in his earphones. He awoke slowly, unbelievingly, hardly understanding the words. "Bart . . ."

"They're gone, John. Back to their hiding places. I guess they decided there was nothing alive down there after all."

John giggled. "I wonder if they were right?"

He heard the voices of the other men coming awake now—puzzled, querulous, or laughing hysterically. Somehow he got to his feet, and with the help of a few fresh men from the ship, rounded up the first shift and got them aboard.

(13)

WORK!

Not since the days of the academy had John pushed himself so hard over a protracted period of time.

Still weak and lethargic from the radiation he'd absorbed on dead Earth, he had to force himself from his bunk after each rationed dollop of sleep. He shaved only so often as his beard became a serious nuisance (for instance, when it was uncomfortable inside a helmet). He spent a lot of time in the radioactive holds of the colossal ship, directing the decontamination and pondering the forthcoming installation of weapons. He ate hastily and dragged himself back to work. He stayed near the dangerous edge of too much radiation—worrying the medics—but he could feel, without any doubt, his steady recovery. He didn't have to prod the men; rather, he had to order them to rest before they collapsed on the job. Their dedication showed in their intent eyes; their gaunt, grim faces; the way they hauled themselves about in free fall (the artificial gravity was off in that part of the ship, to facilitate handling the heavy launchers and rupters and laser clusters harvested from Earth).

Decontamination was tedious, but steady. Thousands of gallons of water spurted out into space. If someone were to rove, within the next few hundred years, through this region of Sparse Space between the spiral arms, he'd wonder at so much radioactivity where hardly a chunk of rock showed on mass detectors. Of course, the chance of anyone breaking out of null at this precise point was tiny.

As each piece of equipment was cleansed down to a tolerable level of "hotness," it was hauled outside the ship (the better to evaporate any lingering wash water) and along the gargantuan hull to a weapons bay near the other end. There were small portable grav units, of course, to supply push where needed; but mostly, men, clinging to the items like ants, used the push of their suits and the strength of their arms and legs. John thought wryly that before this job was finished everyone's biceps would be an inch bigger.

And there was the task, not muscle-straining, but almost overwhelming in the complexity of detail, of wiring the weapons for control. Easy enough to say that the feeding in to a computer of simple arithmetic factors would convert alien mathematical constants to Terran ones, but that stated only the bare basic fact. Every launcher, every rupter, every beamer had to be bore-sighted to aim exactly where fire-control sensors (located, in some cases, five hundred feet from the weapon itself) directed. Every bit of ship's power for the weapons had to be converted from direct current to alternating, and that alternating current run through the frequency multipliers that were integral parts of the weapons themselves.

And the testing—the tedious, maddening testing! After a while Fred Coulter swore that the few missiles being used had developed habits of their own—and knew the way home, like a milk-wagon horse.

But as the hundreds of weary hours dragged by, the number of battle-ready weapons mounted steadily. And the time came when the huge ship could spit out simultaneously a salvo of three dozen heavy missiles, while flashing thirty beams from thirty laser clusters and bringing to bear in various directions twenty-eight heavy rupters. John had planned on thirty of those, too, but a couple turned out to have faulty grav plates that would have allowed serious recoil reaction.

Of course not all the lasers or rupters could be aimed at a single target—they bristled from different sides of the ship. And she was deficient aft. "Aft" became, by some unspoken agreement, the end of the ship where radioactivity still lingered. If that end were ever attacked, it would have to be defended by steerable missiles only, or by the small horde of Armed Scouts that could buzz out of their recesses.

John had not had to cut ports in the big hatch covers, after all—he'd come up with a better idea. Makeshift shields had been erected, from the stock of wonder-metal plates in storage, to close off most of each big hole. That had the added advantage of supplying extra armor *inside* the steel hatch covers.

There was no problem of power. Those immense conduits emerging from the sealed core of the ship could take care of everything—even though they might be clothed in an eerie glow like St. Elmo's fire—without even a slight dimming of ship's lights to show an overload.

Fred Coulter, who, by dint of plain contributed effort, had become ship's engineering officer, worried about that power. "What in hell *is* in that core, anyway? What'll happen if it runs out in the middle of a battle?"

John grinned. "I calculated things out once, assuming that one-tenth the space in there's occupied by fuel metal —copper, to allow even more of a margin for error. It would take about seventeen hundred of steady full operation to deplete it. And according to the Omniarch, the ship was supposed to be in ready condition. We'll just have to hope that 'ready' means completely fueled. What's more likely is that we'll run out of missiles. We ought to have taken a little more time, maybe, and gotten more while we were on Earth. We've got seventy-two heavy missiles, including six erratic ones that can't be counted on except as decoys or feints. Less than two hundred lighter ones for auxiliary fire power and defense. You can't fight a fleet action just with energy weapons—you have to put some missiles around a target to keep it honest."

Coulter nodded. "But we'll be a real dragon against fixed targets!"

"If," John said, "we ever have to show ourselves. I think

we'll avoid it. But Vez Do Han probably has some more definite data on the next targets. I'm going to try to talk him out of a few more missiles, if I can without making him suspicious."

(14)

SECOND PRIME Senior Marshal Bulvenorg peered slit-eyed at the nervous officer seated in the visitor's chair on the other side of the desk. Sometimes the incompetence of subordinates made it hard to maintain one's calm. He laced his strong fingers together and gripped them hard, then unfolded them and laid his hands flat upon the metaloplast surface of his desk. "I find it hard to believe," he said with quiet suppressed fury, "that, after being sent all the way to Sol to set up a watch there, you find it possible to shrug off as an anomaly of instruments the very thing for which you were sent!"

The officer's face suffused with blood. "But, sir! What the instruments we'd planted on Earth indicated is impossible!"

Bulvenorg smiled toothily. "Impossible? I did not realize that you were theoretical physicist, electronics engineer, and theologist all combined into one. But since you are, pray enlighten me. How, impossible?"

The subordinate was obviously finding it hard not to snarl. "A ship twenty-nine hundred *pezras* long? A null from within hardly more than six thousand *pezras* of the planetary surface, where enough atmosphere exists to leak off a full null charge within a fraction of a *sheg?* Surely, sir—" He swallowed, then tried again. "I have the admission of the manufacturer of the recording instrument that emplacement for several hundred *shegs* in radioactivity of that level might cause malfunction. And, since the same instrument recorded, within a fraction of a *sheg*, passage of one of my own ships on patrol—why, it is very clear

that the earlier apparent recording was some kind of
electronic double-registering, with a concurrent error in
magnitude of the readings."

Bulvenorg sighed deeply. "So," he said sweetly, "the
dispatch of eighteen ships to such a distance, and their
deployment over such a period of time, has demonstrated
one thing, clearly, at least: that instrumentation is a waste
of time. For, if a vice-admiral knows so handily which
instrument recordings are valid and which invalid—even
though the instruments have been very carefully chosen by
experts for the particular conditions of that time and place
—why do we not simply let vice-admirals, or perhaps even
second helpers to janitors, sit at home and prognosticate
what the instruments are going to record?"

The officer trembled with rage. "Sir, I appeal to any
competent judge—"

Bulvenorg controlled his own anger and leaned forward
across the desk. "You have already set yourself up as the
judge, in your own mind at least. But let us not waste time
on detours. Did the instrument not record quite properly
the subsequent passages on patrol of several of your own
ships?"

"Yes, but—"

"And did it not yield correct data as to their size, speed,
and altitude?"

"It did, sir. However—"

"And had it not, during your precious patrols over the
planet, worked perfectly?"

The officer stirred in his chair as if he could hardly
keep himself in it.

Bulvenorg spat out, *"True?"*

"True, sir. Sir, if I may speak—"

Bulvenorg spread his arms apologetically. "Pardon me
if I gave you the impression that you did not have permission to speak! Indeed, I have been trying for a quarter of
a *sheg* to get you to utter one word of sense!"

Now the officer actually did snarl, which suited Bulvenorg, for in rage there was truth, and sometimes accurate
recollection. "Sir—Second Prime—as there *are* no ships

and could not *be* any ships of that size, due to limitations of structural materials, it was and is clear to me that the instrument faultily recorded, in partial duplicate, the passage of a ship of mine. And on that I will stand, sir."

"I see. And you say that radioactivity made it malfunction."

"Yes, sir!"

"And was the radioactivity there stronger, or of a different kind, than around other identical instruments?"

The officer flushed again. "Well . . . they were all dropped by parachute. This particular one may have made a harder landing."

"Oh. And such peculiar landing that it malfunctioned just once—although it functioned perfectly before that one instance, and after that one instance. I am afraid, Admiral, that you are a fool. Why did you not land and pick up the instrument for testing? Curse it—would that have been so much of a chore, considering the scope of the mission?"

The officer was becoming unsure of himself now. "Sir, I —that, perhaps, is something I should have done. If we had brought it back with us—or tested it on the spot, to demonstrate its defectiveness . . ."

Bulvenorg sighed. "Admiral, I fear that if you affirm just once more in such a positive way that the instrument was defective, I shall leap out of this chair and bend it around your head."

"But, Second Prime! A ship three thousand *pezras* long—"

"Twenty-nine hundred, you said. By all means, let us not exaggerate *that!* Now, I have replayed half a *vayl* times the recording rod you made of that instrument's report. It clearly records the approach laterally, descent, hovering for some time, hasty rise, and nulling away, *and subsequent return* of a gigantic oblong ship. Did you play over the portion that records the return?"

Now the officer turned almost the color of blood. "Why, sir— My electronics officer . . ."

"Described it to you clearly," Bulvenorg finished for him. "But you said that it was some kind of an 'electronic echo.' That you already knew that particular instrument was defective." He sighed and sat for a moment staring at the officer. "I will admit, Admiral, that I find a ship of that size hard to believe. However, I am confronted here with two things that are even harder to believe. One is that any instrument's malfunctioning could produce such an utterly clear and convincing record. The other is that you—a competent Command Level officer, according to your past history—could listen to such a record and ignore it."

The Admiral was through arguing now. To his credit, he stood up, face wooden, and said in a well-controlled voice, "Sir, I admit that I at no time listened to the complete record myself. I further absolve any and all subordinates. I ask Council Judgment, and accede in advance to any penalty that may be levied."

Bulvenorg smiled. "That will not be for me to decide. You have bungled badly, but personnel evaluation is not my job. Rely on this—you are from this moment no longer attached to the Defense Perimeter. I am sorry, but I cannot cover up this incredible affair. I suggest you ask for immediate retirement. I will lend my endorsement. Good day to you, Admiral, and good luck."

When the blunderer had left, Bulvenorg slumped in his chair for a full twenty-five *centishegs*, thinking hard. Then he reached for the intercom key. "Gusten?"

"Yes, sir."

"Can you step in here a minute? And do you have a bottle?"

A surprised pause. "Yes, I do, Second Prime."

"Bring it with you, if you will. Mine's nearly empty—and I think we shall need more than a sip."

Gusten, his drink sitting on the desk untouched, stared at Bulvenorg. Finally he managed, "You've played the full record rod yourself?"

"Yes; do you want to hear it?"

Admiral Gusten shook his head dazedly. "Later, perhaps. If *you're* convinced . . ."

"I wish to space I weren't! But I am. Curse it—have you

heard anything new lately in the field of high-strength metals?"

"No. And any advance such as—as this implies would be big news!"

"My very thought. Now, let us forget for the moment that we are sane logical beings—if we are—and assume that there *could* be a ship of that size. Who built it?"

Gusten blinked at him for a moment, then sighed limply. "The Klee, of course." He picked up his glass and drained it. "Do you think, Bulvenorg, that that *miant's* nightmare has finally come alive?"

"I fear it. Now, can we tie in the visit of such a ship to Earth—under the very noses of our watch there—with our earlier speculation that the surviving Earthmen are involved in those intrigue raids against the Bizh?"

Gusten sighed. "We can. But I do not like the string."

"Nor I. Well, old classmate, we have lived like *turgs,* and we shall not die like *miants,* eh? I propose that we follow another of our erstwhile hunches."

Gusten grinned and motioned at the bottle, which was sitting closer to Bulvenorg. "They were all your hunches, Second Prime. I claim no credit or blame."

"I will accept both. We were speculating that the raiders might strike next at the far end of the Bizh Empire. So, let us fill the Sparse Regions between ourselves and that locale with whatever surveillance is possible. And let us offer to the Bizh, as an earnest of our innocence, a warning. And furthermore, let us shore up our espionage among the Bizh and among the Hohdans as much as possible. And, of course, we must share this disturbing leap of events with the other services and with the Civilian Government. It is too big—and its implications are too many—to bottle up."

(15)

THE GALAXY as viewed from the Sparse Regions, if for some reason one put on a suit and went outside a ship, was humbling.

This particular occasion was an inspection, from the outside, of the steel hatch cover over one of the bays where a laser cluster had been installed. During testing, a touch of the beam had raked the edge. But a perfunctory look showed that there was no damage.

John, as long as he was out here anyway, clumped around to where he could look both ways (inward and outward) in the plane of the galactic lens.

Outward was the long diffuse spill of the spiral arm occupied by the Vulmot Empire. Farther in along that arm, Sol drifted among his neighbors in the great galactic swirl; but that was two thousand light-years away, and in any case, hidden now by the "aft" end of the ship.

Even at the closest part of the arm, only a few bright stars stood out from the nebulous glow, and those five or six bright ones weren't really *in* the arm, they were along the inner edge of it. There was one bright globular cluster, almost opposite him, that he could place. The Vul home-world was only fifty light-years or so from one edge of that cluster. In the cluster itself was the heaviest concentration of Vul military might, handy to whatever sources of metals and other materials it needed. Wouldn't it be a real hassle, he thought, if the Bizh ever decided to launch raids in that direction! For the Bizh power, though less concentrated, was spread heavily along the nearer edge of the inner spiral arm. That put them somewhere near the middle of their spiral arm—longitudinally—and only a couple of hundred light-years out from the Hohdan region. That made the two empires almost contiguous, as null distances went.

Drongail, where he'd been vaguely expecting, not long ago, to end his life, was in the very base of the Bizh-Hohdan spiral arm—at this moment hidden, like the vicinity of Sol, by the vast bulk of the ship on which he stood. That was the general region into which most of the men had drifted after their first period of employment by Hohd. John thought he understood the vague feelings behind that. They were shunning the spiral arm where dead Earth circled the familiar sun and putting the far-flung bulk of the Hohdan Empire between them and the Vuls.

Humbert Daal and the few who collected around him were exceptions. They'd taken to Sol's spiral arm, despite the relative nearness of the Vuls. Maybe, subconsciously, they'd sought the possibility of quick death. . . .

He grunted to himself. All this rumination. . . . Foolish sophistry. Probably each man drifted where convenience took him.

He tilted his head and looked up at right angles to the galactic plane, into deep lonely space where only a few vagabond stars glittered against the black. If you looked between those terribly isolated stars you could see the dim small ovals that were other galaxies. Did life exist there too? Man would never know. It didn't seem likely that any species of this galaxy, even ten billion years from now, would ever know.

For a few minutes he turned off his suit radio to still the murmur of voices in the earphones. In stark silence, except for the mutter of his own pulse, he stared into the unknowable.

Then he lowered his head and looked toward the galactic center.

He was somewhere near the middle of the Sparse Region between spiral arms, so the pattern of individual stars and clusters looked much the same as in the direction of the Vulmot Empire. But the background of diffuse light was stronger. And, at one point, there was such a solid luminosity (although a dim one) that it looked as if a dense fog had formed there at the center of the galaxy. Maybe there *was* something like a fog—no one knew; no one from this outer sector. The kinds of life existing here could not penetrate inward more than ten or twelve thousand light-years. Radiation and the "gas" of the charged particles were too intense, shorting out electrical circuits no matter how careful the insulation, pouring through the thickest possible bulkheads of selected alloy.

He saw the group he'd led out here turn and clump toward him. He turned on his radio. "How's it look?"

Fred Coulter's voice said, "They all look okay, Commodore. Are we going any farther forward?"

"No. We'll go back in now."

John and Bart Lange pored over a sort of contour map —a representation on paper of an outer region of the Bizh Empire.

John tapped a pencil (of Hohdan manufacture) on a certain area enclosed within an irregular sketched-in oval. "A staging area. It would be used to funnel supplies and reinforcements to any strike outward across the Sparse Regions. The idea is to hit two or three bases and put them out of action for a while—plant long-life fissionables as well as destroying buildings and equipment and ships."

Lange was in a glum mood. "And Bizh."

John looked at him silently for a minute. "Who was it, Bart, who dragged me out of Drongail and bullied me out of the *dron* habit and took me to see the Omniarch?"

Lange gestured irritably. "I'm not saying we should back out. But I don't have to enjoy the killing, do I? Why can't we just feint, and lurk around picking off a few dispatch ships when they break out of null, and whatnot?"

"Because," John said impatiently, "we have to make it realistic. It won't be for long; within a few hundred hours the Bizh and the Vuls will get together one way or another. And before they rush into an all-out war, there'll be meetings and charges and denials and some kind of formal truce which both sides will be very ostentatious about keeping. It won't matter what they *suspect*—they have to consider *all* possibilities. And we don't want to drag things out by pussyfooting around. The sooner the two empires start talking, the sooner our job is ended. Then we can bargain all-out with the Omniarch."

Lange sighed. "I suppose so. But I can't help remembering that we're down to less than two hundred now. . . . What kind of strikes will these be? Low passes, using everything?"

"I think not. That would use up too many small missiles for defense. We won't go close enough to use rupters. We'll null the sixty-thousand-tonner and eight Armed Scouts from within a twentieth light-year—according to Vez Do Han they don't have any picket ships that far out —and break out in a loose cluster within ten miles of the main base. We'll fire one salvo of heavies, programmed for an erratic course in, and send a moderate screen of light stuff ahead of it to saturate the defense. Then we'll take maximum evasive action ourselves, and fight off counterattack with everything we've got—except that if our laser clusters aren't too busy we'll aim them at whatever ground targets are still handy. Then as soon as we're recharged we'll null the hell out of there."

Lange looked bored. It wasn't much different from the first three raids they'd made except that this time they were staying farther off and weren't doing any close-in feinting. "At least," he said, "if we're not going to use lasers right from the start, most of them'll have time to take shelter."

John was silent for a minute. Better not admit that he'd been thinking along those lines himself. Squeamishness wasn't supposed to be an attribute of great generals. And he was playing the part, at least, of mankind's only living great general. Bart asked, "What about *Bertha* and the rest of the Armed Scouts?"

John looked at him quickly. "Bertha?"

Bart grinned tiredly. "We need a name for this behemoth we've got. How about *Big Bertha?* Or *Bertha* for short."

John shrugged. That name would carry through radio static well enough. "You'll be the rescue squad again. We'll rendezvous about a light-year from the base planet and I'll transfer to *Luna.* If nothing shows up to bother you, you'll stay there with the rest of the small ships. You can use that super-mass-detector system you found, and watch for any ambush fleet that breaks out of null near us. If you do see it, and the timing is such that we're not ready to null, you can hop in and throw everything you've got at them. Then, when we're recharged, we'll all bag it back here."

Lange scowled. "I don't like this being the rear echelon all the time."

"Bart, I have to make fast decisions on the firing lines, and I *have* to have someone in reserve I can rely on. If we'd had this setup before, there'd still be a dozen more of us, probably. Now be a good soldier."

"Yeah," the stocky man grumbled, but he didn't argue.

John watched the breakout chronometer needle on *Luna*'s console. He leaned forward and announced (not that anyone would need reminding, but it helped morale), "Fifteen seconds to breakout." He filled his lungs, forced the tenseness in his middle to stay there and not invade his hands, and waited.

Breakout!

Viewscreens flashed to life with sudden images. Points of light glowed suddenly in the mass-detector globe. He gave them a quick look (they all represented his own ships) and let his fingers dance briefly over the main computer keyboard, making a minor but vital change in the preprogramming. Solenoids slammed, transformers hummed, and the images on the viewscreens expanded like explosions. A voice came suddenly from the intercom, "Six. Central control erratic!"

Damn! Something wasn't working right, and one of the small ships wasn't properly locked into the maneuvering formation. "Drop out!" he snapped. "Take position a safe distance behind me, and pilot yourself."

"Wilco," said the voice—Jim Cameron's.

Blips appeared on a screen—a salvo of ground-to-space missiles. John grinned briefly. He could see from the pattern that the local Gunnery Control officer had studied reports of his earlier raids at the other end of the Bizh Empire and was assuming tentatively that this one would follow the same pattern. Well, that assumption would cost the Bizh defense one salvo. . . . He let his eyes rest briefly on a data screen above the main keyboard. Figures began to scroll across it—a playback of the programmed maneuver about to be executed. He could barely hear the clicks and hums as missiles blasted away from *Luna,* but the figures told the story.

Now his instant of firing was finished. The beautifully tuned drives and artificial grav made the sudden maximum deceleration and the sharp swerve to the side almost imperceptible, though he was waiting for the faint sensation. He shot a look at one particular screen to make sure Cameron was following the maneuver. He was. The little fleet twisted back and away like a frantically dodging hare. And it was a good thing—a swarm of blips filled the mass-detector globe now, G-to-S missiles streaking furiously toward him. Gunnery officers and men of his various ships were grunting and cursing to themselves now as they punched computers and in some cases slammed manual controls around, setting up the defense. The ships were dancing, darting, as they went, to make poorer targets for heavy ground-based energy beams. John's pulses pounded with the elation of making the enemy look like a fool. Dials showed him that practically all his laser clusters were busy spitting frightful heat at ground targets big enough to be worthwhile. Even if only a few of the beams slashed across buildings, the damage would be enough to make the base commander howl with rage. If Bizh howled.

A klaxon blasted, and his eyes flashed to the mass detector. He drew in his breath sharply. An enemy fleet—just breaking out of null, almost within fighting range! No surprise, really—the Bizh would certainly have been prepared—and not a real danger, since he was almost ready to null. Still . . .

He gasped suddenly and shouted into the intercom, "Six! Cameron! Get in close to me!"

Cameron's calm voice said, "Coming, John."

But John was cursing himself, in agony at his own slow wits. With maneuvering like this, Cameron daren't pilot his ship too close to the others—nor could his computer, cut off from the others, help him. And out there, several miles from the group, where he couldn't share the group's defensive swarm of small missiles, he was a prime target! John's few moments of forgetfulness might make the critical difference.

The klaxon, which had shut itself off as preprogrammed to do, now bleated again. John had to throw looks at several screens before he could be sure that the new alarm was what he hoped; then he let out his breath in relief. A data screen showed a distance and direction and mass that could only be *Bertha*. Bart was here.

Or almost here. There would still be a large fraction of a minute before *Luna* or the Armed Scouts could null or before they and the huge ship could join for common firepower. And, anyway, he had no intention of nulling to safety and leaving Bart to fight alone while recharging for null.

So, out John went, weaving, feinting, not needing to tell anyone what to use the lasers for now. The enemy fleet was fairly closely massed, less than ten miles away, jumping about in an effort to stay in his path. Viewscreens lit with dazzling light, went dark, came on again with normal images, flared out again. This was a real bit of infighting! Seconds dragged. Still John punched at the keyboard, inventing the most unlikely maneuvers, striving to be as evasive as physically possible yet still put more distance, by crazy increments, between him and the Bizh fleet. Thank God the computer lock-in was holding together, except for Cameron! And Cameron was following *Luna* as closely as any man could, putting himself to the rear when possible, coming riskily close to other ships now and then, but not foolhardily close.

Now missiles from *Bertha* began reaching the enemy. Almost immediately the pressure on John lessened. He tried to follow the enemy's evasive reactions, anticipate them, so he could get a good lead to one side and hold it. He wanted to be well out of line when Bart's lasers were in effective range.

Then, suddenly, the screens went dazzling white again, and at the same moment, or a split second before, someone shouted incoherently on the radio. The deafening, stunning noise of a direct hit—heard from inside the stricken ship —came over the radio for just an instant before it was chopped off. John squeezed his eyes shut for a moment, drew in a shuddering breath, and fought to stay calm. Another voice from the radio shouted, "Six is gone! Damn them—they—" John snapped, "All right, Damiano—get hold of yourself!"

He forced his eyes to the viewscreens again. The enemy was in utterly defensive flight now. John had no trouble in arcing around them and darting swiftly toward *Bertha*. The enemy—had they known it—surely carried ten times the firepower of *Bertha, Luna,* and all the small ships combined. But John didn't blame him for running. He'd have run too, suddenly confronted with an impossibly huge object, bristling with weapons, and at least five escorting units. How could the Bizh know that twenty or thirty of the monsters wouldn't break out of null any second?

Listlessly, John looked up at a dial. He could null now, and *Bertha* would be ready in less than two minutes. But it didn't matter. The enemy fleet was far out of fighting range, and so was the planetary base. There was no talk on the intercom, until John called *Bertha* and said, "Bart, you may as well take aboard all the small ships and null them to rendezvous with you."

Bart was not only upset about the death of Cameron and seven other men but also nervous about something that showed on *Bertha*'s from-null detector system. "That's a group of ships," he said, pointing to it, "somewhere within a few billion miles. They show on the instrument, vanish from it—appearing on that other system that shows them in normal space—stay for five minutes, then show in null again. They move about a twentieth of a light-year each time. That's why I was a little slow in coming to join you—I delayed for about a minute, watching them. It looks as if they're running a search pattern. They moved twice while we were fighting that skirmish, and again while you were transferring from *Luna*."

John watched the detector system listlessly. "They're probably Vuls, though they might be Bizh. The Vuls have done more here in the Sparse Regions." He didn't care either way. What mattered, just now, was that Cameron was gone, and seven other good men. How many did that leave now? One hundred and eighty-three? He swallowed, and swallowed again. God; if he only had a *muzhee* of *dron*. . . . Fleetingly his mind toyed with the subterfuge of running down to Jessa—saying he wanted to know whether the Vuls had hit it or not, actually, though, to try to find some *dron*. He fought the notion with all his tired will and forced his mind to other things. "We've got to make at least one raid farther out along this arm. Let's do it right away and get it over with. For now, we'd better get out of here, if there's a search pattern going on. We'll run out to near where we'll be raiding."

Bart looked at him expressionlessly. "In Sparse Space? Or should we go somewhere in the arm, beyond the Bizh?"

"In Sparse Space, I'm afraid. Our maps and data aren't good enough to go blundering around in the arm. Say, an hour's hop from here—no; that's a period of time the Vuls might think of if they already suspect us. Seventy-nine minutes. Break out and look around." He sat down wearily in the pilot's seat and punched out a program.

Then he got to his feet and started toward the chemical lab they'd set up. There'd be plenty of grain alcohol there. Mix it with water and a little glycerin or something. If he couldn't get *dron*, the next best thing for this awful thirst-

that-was-not-thirst would be to get drunk and sleep it off.
The men needed eight or ten hours' rest anyway before
the next (and, he intended, the *last*) strike. Bart could
stand watch meanwhile.

(16)

JOHN SAT with Bart in *Bertha*'s big control room. He felt a little muzzy from the drinking he'd done a few hours before, but the *dron* thirst was down to a bearable level.

"I've been pondering," he said, "how the Bizh have got that ambush system set up. And how this ship's detector systems can outsmart it." He paused, glancing at the instruments in question. "They must keep at least two task forces ready not far from each important base."

Bart looked puzzled. "Why more than one?"

"Because," John said, "you can't keep a ship charged for null more than a few hours, without the charge leaking off. And if you're on standby, you want to be ready *all* the time. So—there are twin forces. One stays charged as long as it can. Safely before the limit, the other charges itself."

Bart looked embarrassed. "Of course. I wasn't thinking."

John grinned. "All right. Anyway, at some point within a very few light-years—or maybe less than one—there's a fleet ready to hop in to support the base at any moment. When we break out of null, the base sends off a dispatch drone—they have those charged and waiting, too, of course—to the position of the standby fleets. And, having exact coordinates, a fleet can null to within fighting range of the base."

Bart raised his eyebrows. "Yes, that's all logical. What does it have to do with *Bertha*'s long-range detector system?"

John told him, "It's a matter of exact timing. All three ambushes we've run into have had about the same time lag in being triggered. About two minutes, from the time we broke out until the time the enemy fleet broke out. That was the time it took to program data into the drones—automatically, I'm sure—null the drones to the standby fleet, transmit the data immediately on breakout, and get the fleet nulled back to the base. Two minutes, more or less."

Bart considered. "That doesn't sound unreasonable, if they have everything ready."

"Right. Now, our minimum attack time is, say, four and a half minutes. We break out, toss everything, recharge for null, and vanish. Using all the weapons diverts enough power from null charge to make it four and a half minutes instead of four."

Bart nodded.

John continued, "If we knew where those standby fleets were, we could pick out an ideal point for breakout. Let's assume, because it's logical, that the ambush fleet is going to break out on the side of the planet where the base is located. If their hideout is on the opposite side of the planet, then they've nulled through or past the planet, and they break out with velocity going *away* from the planet, and have to decelerate. If they come from somewhere on the same side of the planet as the base, then they'll break out moving *toward* the planet, and still have to decelerate. In either case, they're busy for a few seconds, at least."

Bart was interested now. "And if they come from the side—that is, tangential to the planet at the point of the base—they'll still have a velocity. And if we know where they're coming from, we can predict their direction of travel when they break out!" He got to his feet and went to stare at the spring-mounted panel. "We can locate them from null. And if we make our strike from close in—*we* can break out close to the planet too, with this gadget—and go in the opposite direction from what *they'll* be going, they can't even start a tail chase until they've decelerated!"

John grinned again. "Not the *opposite* direction; that might put us on a collision course. And even if we dodged actual collisions, there'd be a close-passing swipe. We don't want that. But there'll always be some optimum course or courses for us. If we hit the base immediately upon break-out, then into that course, they'll never get near us!"

Bart was grinning now too. "Not the next strike, any-way. If we made more, they might be smart enough to delay sending off that drone until they see which way we're turning."

John said, "We could always turn twice. Anyway, this is going to be the last strike. Now, there's one problem."

"What?"

"Well," John said, "the ambush fleet can travel eight light-years per minute in null, or thirty-two to thirty-six in the time it takes us to null away after the strike. Halving that distance—because the drone has to get to them—we get sixteen light-years. Allow a few seconds lost for mes-sages to be transmitted and recorded, and for relays to close and for animal reaction—unless it's a hundred per-cent automatic—and you might say the standby point could be anywhere within twelve light-years of the base. I don't suppose these super eyes of *Bertha*'s can see a fleet that far?"

"Lord, no," Bart said. "I've b--- ~guring, tentatively, between one and two light-years."

John nodded. "So we could grow long white beards trying to locate them in a volume of space with a radius of twelve light-years. There is one thing, though; they won't null through the planet's star unless they're desperate enough to run a five- or six-percent risk of getting thrown completely off course by null distortion. If we make our strike, then turn directly toward the sun—or a little to one side of it—we'll at least know that we aren't on collision courses. And we want to hit the base in daylight anyway. Now, if Vez Do Han's data aren't completely wrong . . ."

The attack went off very smoothly as planned.

This was a dry, sandy world, about seven thousand miles in diameter, with (instruments said during their brief glimpse) a fairly large iron core. Surface appearance confirmed that: the soil whether it was the wide stretches of sand corrugated with wind drifts or the nearly bare, eroded-down mountains, showed reddish tinges that were undoubtedly iron oxide. The oceans were tiny, and there were few rivers. Vegetation was very sparse, and all of it was an ugly olive-brown color. Atmosphere, so far as instruments could calculate from outside it, was less than ten pounds per square inch at "sea level" and contained only about eight percent oxygen. The buildings, photos showed later, were all pressurized. There seemed to be no native animal life and no Bizh civilian villages. John, leading the attack as usual in *Luna,* was glad of that—because they really clobbered the place.

They broke out of null less than four thousand feet above the biggest concentration of buildings. That was lower than John had planned—and extremely risky, because the null charge *might* not have been able to shunt aside any more air than actually existed. However, it did—and the surface must have shivered with sonic booms. Salvos of missiles leaped away immediately. The intercom was a chaos of muttering and cursing as gunners pitted human senses and reaction speed against the capabilities of their rupters and laser clusters.

The viewscreens were full of images darting and turning too fast for John to follow; but most of what they showed, to the groundward side, was pure hell. In the ten square miles of the main base, eighteen or twenty medium-sized ships were caught on the ground and were either blasted to shards or so badly damaged that salvage wouldn't be worthwhile. Hangars were flattened.

Within seventy seconds the attack was finished and they were flashing away from the planet and already out of fighting range.

And John, slowly punching keys to bring taped movies of the thing onto viewscreens, felt sick.

In addition to the grounded ships—just a few looked still intact—he'd knocked down eighty percent or more of the buildings here. And those buildings had been pressurized. Could surviving Bizh live, breathing only this miserable planet's atmosphere? He hoped so. For there were always survivors, dazedly crawling out from under not quite flat walls, or from compartments of hull-shattered ships, or from underground shops and barracks.

The intercom was strangely silent. He supposed the men felt the same way he did. A fight was a fight, but this sudden slaughter was another thing entirely.

He swallowed hard. Well, the Bizh species wasn't threatened. There were plenty of Bizh away from military bases.

He was glad there'd been so few ships on the ground. The Bizh commanders must really be scared by now— probably they sent nine-tenths of their ground-based fleets into hiding. He could imagine crews grumbling bitterly at having to spend so much time in space. Well, they should be glad they hadn't been here!

And the planet hadn't been any resort world, anyway.

He swallowed again, and looked at the chronometer. Less than two minutes to null.

And it was another minute before a large number of blips suddenly appeared on the screen. They gave chase, but he was accelerating fast toward the planet's star, and they'd come in from the side and weren't going to get near enough to worry him even a little. They did launch a salvo, but that was pure, enraged spite. Then they turned back to do what they could for the base.

He kept swallowing. *It's just the one base,* he told himself insistently. *Only a fraction of the planet's garrison. And they have so many other planets.*

Nevertheless, if there'd been any *dron* aboard, he'd have chewed it right then. He did hurry out of the Control Room (with the two lieutenants staring silently and expressionlessly after him) for a healthy slug of liquor before they broke out at rendezvous. He couldn't help equating the planet he'd just left with Earth.

There were blips in *Bertha*'s detection spheres again, nulling, breaking out into n-space, and nulling again. John, his nerves in bad shape, reached irritably for the keyboard.

Bart watched him silently for a minute, then asked, "Are we nulling back toward Hohd?"

John gave him a distracted look. "Not immediately. I'm damned if we're going to make any more strikes for Hohd, but I promised Vez we'd do a little scouting out here before we leave. We won't do it the way he expects— by breaking out of null close enough to certain targets to put telescopes on them and set up radio listening; we'll just use *Bertha*'s systems to pinpoint Bizh concentrations of ships and planetary systems they seem to be based in. That's the information he wants. He doesn't have to know how we get it."

Bart looked sour. "How long will all that take? It's been a long time since we set foot on a planet."

John told him impatiently, "An extra twenty hours, maybe. We can stand it." But he swallowed hard, and wondered.

The actual reconnaissance of Bizh power took less than that. However, there was a mystery that they came across, far out in the Sparse Regions—beyond any Vul outpost and almost beyond the Bizh influence—that caused them to spend almost the full twenty hours before starting "home."

The blip began to show on the from-null detector system, at extreme range, before they made their first stop to spy briefly on a concentration of ships. They mapped that star-and-planet system without emerging from null. As they moved on, the strange blip crept slowly in from the edge of the transparent. It was a purple-blue blip—intense enough to represent a very large star, except that they'd never seen that color used before.

"Whatever it is," Bart muttered, fiddling with knobs, "we're still four hundred and ten light-years from it, as well as I can calculate."

John walked over to stand beside him. "Maybe a star with something special about it. We still haven't any idea how this wizard's gadget works. Maybe the Klee could tell when a star was about to nova, or something else dangerous about it."

Bart shrugged. "Do you think we ought to go have a closer look, as long as we're out here?"

John pondered that. He was impatient to be turned

around and headed "home." Still, an unknown phenomenon ought not to be ignored. "I guess so. We haven't seen
any more of that Vul search pattern, if it was one. We can
break out, say, within ten light-years of this thing and have
a look. If it's an incipient nova, we'll still be safe by a big
margin."

However, it was not an incipient nova. It wasn't even a
star. They broke out of null; saw the thing, still represented by purplish-blue light, on the Klee system of detection for n-space; and found nothing in the telescopes. They
went closer, in four cautious hops. Finally, by Bart's calculation, they were within one light-year. Still they could see
nothing.

And when they made another short hop, not without
nervousness, there was still nothing. Ordinary mass detectors should show it now, if it were as big as a washtub.
John frowned over the instruments for a minute, then
suddenly walked to his seat and began punching out a
program. Then he leaned toward the intercom. "Damiano?"

From somewhere the communications officer (and
commander of one of the Armed Scouts) answered, 'Les,
Commodore?"

"We've got some kind of a blip about a quarter of a
million miles from us. Get your crew aboard Number
Seven, will you, and go out and look for it? I'll give you the
vector as soon as we spit you out."

"Yes, sir."

John waited. Instruments told him when the men, suited
up, boarded the Armed Scout in the airless hold. They
informed him when the big hatch cover slid open and
when the small ship left. *Bertha* didn't actually "spit them
out"—they left under their own power—but the expression had caught on.

Damiano's voice came over the radio. "We're outside,
Commodore."

John punched a stud to feed the direction vector to the
small ship's computers.

A minute passed. Then Damiano reported puzzledly,

"We don't have any blip on our screens, sir."

John blinked in surprise, then looked up at a radar screen. It hadn't shown anything, of course, during their cautious approach—distances, short in null, had still been far too great in n-space.

And the screen showed nothing now.

Frowning, he programmed a question for the computer. An answer scrolled across the data screen: *The object shown on special detector systems is not a radar object.*

He stared at the screen, then scowled down at the offending keyboard. There were still difficulties, from time to time, because he had to use English, which the computer didn't handle perfectly yet. He turned to the intercom grille and told Damiano, "Stay where you are for a minute." Then he put another question to the computer: "What is the blip that was the subject of the last question?"

The answer was plain enough: *The blip shows position of a marker.*

John stared. The word "marker" was certainly part of the computer's English vocabulary. With an errie feeling, he punched the question: "Is the marker a Klee artifact?"

Yes.

John sighed. "Damiano, did you hear that?"

"I did, Commodore. Do you want me to go look at it?"

"Yes, Luis, but be careful."

"Yes, sir."

Damiano must have been careful, for it was nearly half an hour before his voice came over the radio again. "Commodore, there is nothing here. And we still have no blips on our radar, and none on the mass detector."

"All right, Luis, come on back." By then John and Bart had switched *Bertha*'s mass-detector system to the ordinary one. It would have showed an object of any size to speak of at that distance. It didn't.

Nor did further questioning of the computer clear up the mystery. The computer's idiot-genius brain accepted the existence of the blip, said it showed the position of a marker, and agreed that there was nothing material at the spot.

Finally Bart shrugged. "Well, it's just a notation in the ship's systems, then—including the computers. Why don't we quit worrying about it?"

John agreed. But he puzzled about it, and did worry a little, all through the many-hours-long journey back to the Hohd region.

(17)

BULVENORG AND GUSTEN sat listening to a newly elevated officer of their Intelligence Vector. This person, thought Bulvenorg, showed a keen and flexible mind.

The man handed each of them sketches of what was presumably a spaceship five or six times as long as it was thick. A simple circle represented the cross section. Top and side drawings were identical; they showed a long hull, rounded at the ends, with circular markings arranged in bands around it at intervals. "This, sirs, is drawn from a verbal description by an actual witness. He said there were about twenty bands of circles around it—I use the word 'bands,' although I believe the actual meaning of the Bizh word is more like 'belts' or 'necklaces,' formed of links and encircling something—and that each band included many circles, not abutting one another but separated by at least the equivalent of their radii. These circles, he said (and perhaps the word should be 'disks'; there is no differentiation in Bizh), were of a darker color than the hull, which seemed smooth and continuous except for the circles. He saw no exterior sensors or other projections. Of course, sirs, as you will realize, at his distance from the ship he could hardly see objects or markings with a diameter of less than, say, twice the height of a Vulmot. I have determined that the Bizh eyes are good, a trifle superior to our own." He paused and let them look at the sketches for a moment. "This account would have us believe that the ship boasted three hundred or more circular hatches, some or all of which might be weapons ports. The witness states that not more than thirty of them, all near one end, opened to expose weapons. They were orthodox types—missile launchers, rupters, laser clusters. The acceleration of the ship appeared fully equal to that of his own. However, he said—I cannot judge the accuracy of this—that the vessel seemed to recharge for null in somewhat less time than his. As you know, the Bizh ships are approximately equal to ours in those two abilities."

Bulvenorg decided to offer this person a drink after all. He reached down, pulled open the desk drawer, and brought out a bottle and three glasses. "Fine; fine! And he judged that the ship might be thirty-five hundred *pezras* long?"

"That is how his figures translate. He admits, though, that due to surprise and to slight damage that his ship suffered, his range finders and photographic equipment did not manage to fix upon the ship during the brief encounter. He says he could be off by an appreciable fraction." He accepted the drink. "Thank you, sir."

Bulvenorg grinned at Gusten. "An estimate of thirty-five hundred *pezras* for a ship twenty-nine hundred *pezras* long. The Bizh are not as phlegmatic and unimaginative as some of us thought, eh?" He looked again at the Intelligence officer. "What did your spy have to say about the smaller ships that his force was beleaguering before the big ship appeared?"

"His account, sir, matches earlier ones very well. A *layl* of our Armed Scouts, plus one of our capital ships—forty-thousand-*lohm, nave* class."

"And," Bulvenorg asked, "they recovered no corpses from the one Armed Scout they destroyed that they could identify as to species?"

"Unfortunately not, sir. To describe the protein matter collected, he used a word that indicates meat chopped up into small particles for food. And already cooked."

"Mm. A pity, for us as well as for the victims. No personal artifacts?"

"Artifacts, sir, that in his opinion might have belonged to almost any humanoid."

Bulvenorg sighed. "Thank you, Second Vector Prime."

He sipped a little of his drink, wondering if he should voice the thought in his mind. He decided he would. "Second, it impinges upon me that you have been very successful in subverting a Bizh ship commander. It has not been our experience that such a thing is easy."

The officer looked a little embarrassed. "I must confess, sir, that this individual undoubtedly conceives of his activity on my behalf more as liaison than as spying."

Bulvenorg straightened a little in his chair. Gusten made a small sound that might indicate amusement. "Do you mean, Second," Bulvenorg asked the officer slowly, "that you have led a Bizh combat officer to think that the Vulmot Empire has accepted him as an envoy-without-credentials?"

The officer colored a little. "I could put it less succinctly, sir, but I fear there is a flavor of that sort in his thinking. I assure you I have not pretended to represent the empire. I confided in him that the ships making the earlier attacks were *not* crewed by Vulmoti nor by mercenaries of Vulmot. And that my interest, though I was pursuing it clandestinely for various reasons, was in avoiding misunderstanding between our empires."

Bulvenorg chuckled. "A very adroit defense of your action. Tell me—in confidence—am I right in an impromptu guess that this individual is secretly in the Bizh Intelligence Service, and that the two of you have exchanged useful information before?"

The officer colored more deeply, but grinned. "Yes. I hope you will understand that, to make contacts at all with such an alien species, we must accept what is available. And I can negotiate with, shall I say, an opposite number of myself—a *turg* of my own stripe—with more discretion than if he were primarily concerned with some different activity."

This time Gusten laughed aloud. Bulvenorg suppressed his own grin. "That, Second," he said seriously, "is quite interesting. As a matter of fact, I have been vaguely hoping that some arrangement of this sort might be worked out. You see, while I am *almost* certain that this ear singeing the Bizh are suffering is not the work of some devious group in one of our own military vectors, I cannot go to the government with that assurance until I have absolute proof. Therefore, though a diplomatic exchange is badly needed, one is hardly possible yet." He eyed the Vector Second Prime for a moment. "Could this opposite number of yours, do you think, quietly reach their military high command? You could use my name, unofficially. I would like to compare suspicions."

The officer blinked. "Sir, I cannot be sure how such an under-the-table arrangement might be greeted by the Bizh high command. But I will put it up to my contact. Will you draft a specific message?"

"I will," Bulvenorg said. "But now, for the moment, there are other matters you have to report, I think."

"Yes, sir. On the subject of Vulmot-built ships in the Armed Scout class. We have abstracted archives dealing with losses, explained and unexplained, during the last ten *megashegs*. We correlated the figures with the presence of Chelki, and find, sir, that in more than sixty percent of the cases Chelki were aboard."

Bulvenorg almost leaped out of his chair. "Sixty percent! That is damning!" He stared at the officer. "And what about the last *megasheg* only? Do you have corresponding figures?"

"Yes, sir. Fifty-eight percent."

Slowly Bulvenorg sat down. He sighed. "I don't suppose you happen to have at your fingertips percentages of all deep-space voyages by Armed Scouts in which Chelki were aboard?"

The officer smiled. "I have. Obviously those figures are of interest. Twenty-two percent."

Bulvenorg slowly looked over at Gusten. Gusten, face serious, abstractedly made the negative sign of thumb to little finger.

Bulvenorg asked another question of the Intelligence officer. "How many Armed Scouts lost and not accounted for during the last ten *megashegs?*"

"Seventy-one, sir."

Bulvenorg felt as if he'd been clubbed. "All right," he mumbled. "One thing more. What about capital ships of the *nave* class?"

"*Nave* class, sir? Four lost and never seen again in the last *megasheg*. One sent off a message drone saying there was malfunction in the null-charging system. Of the other three, only one was the forty-thousand-*lohm* class. That was a new ship, sir, on its shakedown cruise. Chelki technicians were aboard."

Bulvenorg got up again and walked twice across the room and back. He stopped, staring at nothing for a moment, then came back to his chair and sat down. "Give me all those statistics in printed form as soon as you can. Now—the matter of Chelki uprisings. I asked you to go into that also. Do you have equally startling facts in that regard?"

"I very much fear I may have, sir. As you know, a certain number of Chelki do vanish now and then—as do Vulmoti, for that matter. But the number of Chelki vanishing in remote regions—on long commercial trips, for instance—is far out of proportion." He paused. "Through application of probability analysis, we actually turned up an individual—a Full Male—who was almost certainly involved in some sort of furtive organization engaged in falsifying records to cover up Chelki disappearances. He may have been involved in the theft of ships, too!"

Bulvenorg closed his eyes for a moment. A very disturbing pattern was beginning to take shape in his mind. He opened his eyes, sighed, and looked at the Intelligence officer for a long moment. Then he asked in a low voice, "What, Second Prime, would you say to the possibility that a considerable number of those escaped Chelki have gathered together somewhere? That, in fact, a viable free colony of them exists and is active against us?"

"That is conjecture, sir. Unfortunately the individual we turned up killed himself before he could be interrogated to a worthwhile degree. You know how those Full Males can produce hormones within themselves. But all in all, I would say the possibility is quite strong. In fact, unofficially, without putting it in writing, I would say very probable!"

Bulvenorg asked no more questions for a while; he simply sat and thought. Then he made the sign of affirmation, smiled grimly at the two Vulmoti with him, and said, "This must go into government hands, of course. But discreetly."

(18)

THE ARMED SCOUT carrying John broke out of null near the planet Akiel, drew the proper response to a radioed password, and landed.

The first thing the senior lieutenant in charge of the small contingent of men left here told John was, "Commodore, there's trouble. Jessa's been raided by the Vuls!"

John looked at him wearily. "That's too bad, but I'm not surprised. When did you hear?"

"A couple of days ago. One of those Bizh ships we were refitting here hopped out to that planet the Hohdans gave you. It was ready for duty. The men there had gotten the word from the Hohdans." He eyed John worriedly. "Does that mean the Vuls may be looking for us here too?"

John told him, "I don't see why; we didn't tell them there was such a planet as Akiel. What about the men who stayed on Jessa? Were they captured?"

"Hohd didn't know that. They only heard about the raid indirectly, from a cargo ship of some small empire that stopped there to pick up a load of fiber. The Vuls hit the human compound but didn't bother anyone else. After they were gone, someone went over for a look, found signs of fighting, but no signs of live men and no human corpses. The natives were disorganized. Some were bringing in fiber and piling it up, but they couldn't say anything coherent."

John brooded about the thing. Well, it didn't make any difference that he could see; his next step was still to see the Omniarch as soon as possible. "Did you put everyone here on full alert?"

"I did, Commodore. I told the Full Male here about it too, of course. He said he'd send word to the Omniarch."

"All right, Lieutenant. I'm going to look up the Full Male myself, right now."

It took the rest of that day and part of the next to find the Full Male. He listened silently to John's request, then said, "Co-mo-dore, I have not heard anything from my ancestor for eight days. I sent him a message about another matter. I expected an answer to that, two days, maybe three days, past. The news your man told me about a planet called Jessa makes me worry that my ancestor may be in trouble too."

John muttered an exasperated curse. "Well, will you try anyway? Send word that I want to see him, urgently?"

"I will, John Braysen. But this we must fear too: if my ancestor is not in trouble, still the chain of—of messages between me and him may be broken. And then I shall have to think for myself of the safety of this planet."

John said, "Of course. Are you hinting that you may place restrictions upon *us?*"

"No, John Braysen, that I cannot do. But I ask you to be —to be dis-creet."

John tried not to scowl. "Of course. But I think we've completed a phase of the Omniarch's plan."

"I will send that word by the only way I know. Will you wait here for a possible reply?"

"No—I have to see a Hohdan commander. As you know, there's a place where the Omniarch and I have made rendezvous before. I'll keep someone on watch there constantly."

"That word too I will send, Co-mo-dore."

Vez Do Han frowned thoughtfully. "No, I can't offer even a guess as to where the Omniarch might be hiding. He is a physically hardy creature, John Braysen, and he could take refuge on almost any chlorophyll-and-protein planet, even a quite primitive one. And, having stayed hidden from the Vulmot Empire as long as he has, I would think him quite sagacious in the ways of a fugitive." Vez smiled. "For instance, he has never even told me where Akiel is, though I can make some broad guesses."

John sighed. "Thank you anyway. Have you had time to read the report I sent about our raids out near the other end of the Bizh Empire?"

"I have." Vez picked up a small model of a spaceship that served as a paperweight on his desk and hefted it idly in one hand. He looked at John for a moment. "As you know, old comrade-in-arms, the Hohdan Empire enjoys the virtues of a democracy—and suffers some of the failings. Thus, at the moment, my superiors are in something of a bind. Though top government officials approved this small ploy we mounted against the Bizh advance, they've now begun to paddle in the opposite direction. I am ordered to divorce myself from it at once—and specifically to sever all connections with human and other mercenaries at once."

John said nothing for a moment. Then, "As you know from my report, we're quite ready to sever the connection ourselves. But I hope your orders do not include a requirement that you repudiate our agreement about that planet in your region—the one where we're planning to settle."

Vez made a disgusted gesture. "My orders would quite clearly include that. However, I have thought of a way to pretend to misinterpret them—and I will *not* order you off that planet. But you may not count on the backing of my superiors, should you be discovered there. Consequently—I advise the utmost discretion."

Vez Do Han's gallantry sent a pang of guilt through John. Here he was playing underhanded with a real friend. . . . "I appreciate your integrity, Vez Do Han. It will put you in an uncomfortable situation."

Vez looked scornful. "I do not care. In any case, this flap about mercenaries will not last long. Some sort of intrigue is cooking constantly, for every big empire; and the Bizh and the Vulmoti will be thinking of other things."

They sat looking at each other uneasily for a while. Then Vez broke the uneasy silence. "Comrade, though our contacts with the Bizh are indirect, a few do exist. And through one spy channel comes a very strange report."

For just a moment John felt a sinking sensation, then suddenly he was grinning. This was a *relief*.

Vez went on, "I know you are an honorable man, John Braysen. I also know that the most honorable of men—like the most honorable of any other species—will do what he must for sufficiently compelling unselfish reasons." He paused, and he was grinning too, and looking excited. "The report told of a very large ship—an impossible one, for any present technology. But the circumstances tie in so prettily with your raids out there . . ." He breathed deeply. "I, too, have a species to which I am loyal. All I ask at this moment is this: if you can see any way we might make our loyalties run parallel, please consider taking that way!"

John laughed. "Yes, comrade, I have a very large ship! You can guess, of course, where I got it. And you can guess that it is Klee. Now, here's the situation—you mention loyalty to my species. You mean, I'm sure, the safety of my few surviving fel'   men, so long as they may last. But there is more th   at." He paused, getting hold of his own feelings. "My ecies does not have to die, Vez Do Han. There are a number of living women—females—hidden somewhere."

He watched the cycle of expressions on the Hohdan face. Startlement, dumbfoundment, excitement, amusement. The last of those broke out into the loud Hohdan laughter. "Don't tell me the rest, John Braysen—allow me to guess! The Omniarch alone knows where they are. And it was he who had you reclaimed from Drongail—from *dron*—and who helped you gather together the other men. Ha, ha! How neatly he has braided this thing together!"

Vez suddenly turned serious. "I see now, John Braysen, how little freedom of choice you actually had. Nevertheless, I am still a loyal Hohdan. Tell me—for the love of space, tell me!—how our loyalties can coincide!"

John took a deep breath. "This way: when we have those women safe from wherever that four-legged schemer hid them, and settled on some planet far away from the Vulmoti, then you can take the cursed ship! Come with me before then, if you like, see it, learn to operate it. My species is so small now, even at best, and has had such a good scare, that we shall want nothing to do with space for a long time. Just some comfortable planet, a backward place, a backwater of this galactic vector. We'll be overwhelmed with joy, I think, even to go back to the beast-power stage!"

Vez was on his feet, trembling with eagerness. "Is this a pact, John Braysen?"

"It's a pact! And if any of my men grumble about it, I'll point out the necessities to them. And it'll be too late to renege anyway!"

(19)

THE HOHDAN unarmed dispatch ship, a small type of vessel easily recognizable by its concave ends (so shaped to accommodate a special kind of grav shieldplate), broke out of null among the stars of the double binary. A quick glance at the mass-detector globe told John that, as planned, his sixty-thousand-ton flagship *Luna* was here ahead of him to explain the sudden appearance of a Hohdan ship—which would otherwise have been more than dismaying to Bart Lange aboard *Bertha*.

He looked at Vez Do Han. "Well, there she is."

Vez may not have heard him at all. The Hohdan was sitting rigidly erect, gaze glued to the viewscreen that showed the huge ancient ship. The humanoid's lips moved silently. Then he drew a ragged breath and turned to John. "Space, comrade! It is as you described her. But no description could have prepared me for this!"

John grinned. "She *is* overwhelming, isn't she? I regret you weren't with us to see her rise up out of a planet's crust. Well, let's move in and transfer aboard." He leaned toward the communicator grille before him.

But before he could radio Bart Lange, Bart's urgent voice came from the receiver. "Is John Braysen aboard? John?"

"Yes, Bart. I'm here with Vez Do Han and four of his specialists."

"John, something's come up! The Full Male from Akiel sent one of our ships out here with a message. Ralph Cole brought it, and he says the Full Male almost clobbered him when he refused to give the coordinates of this place. But they finally agreed upon Ralph's promise to get to you, no matter what." John could hear Bart inhale deeply. "The Omniarch's in bad trouble. The Vuls broke his spy chain and are hunting him down, or trying to. He's hiding on the planet where you and he dug up *Bertha*. The Vuls don't know yet that he's there, but they know he *has* been there, before, and they're watching the planet in case he shows up. He has no ship and no means of survival for more than a short time. He asks whether you can rescue him— he doesn't think the Vuls have much of a force in the region. He says he has a way of communicating with you when you get there, if you can chase out the Vuls." Lange paused again. "Cole says the Full Male and the rest of the Akiel colony are like a bunch of crazy-mad hornets. He says he never knew a Chelki could act like they're acting."

John stared at the receiver grille. "How long ago did Cole reach you?"

"About seven hours ago. He's not here now; he insisted on nulling out right away for that planet we're supposed to settle on, if . . . when we're through with everything else."

John glanced at the Hohdan. "Bart, I've told Vez Do Han about the women. He's an ally in that now."

There was a long pause. When Bart's voice came again, it conveyed his shock and disapproval. "Well, that's where Cole went to try to find you. He practically told me to go to hell when I wanted to keep him here and send someone else in his place. Said he'd given the Full Male his word and wasn't going to break it for anything. They must have really scared him on Akiel!"

John's mind churned, and a familiar cold lumpiness was in his middle. "Cole's right in being scared. Damn it, Bart, everything depends on the Omniarch. Look—we're coming aboard. Meanwhile, send dispatch drones around to gather every man we've got, as fast as they can make it here. We'll have to run out to that planet we were going to settle on, if we ever found the women, and get all the munitions stockpiled there. Then we'll go rescue the Omniarch. Did the Full Male offer any direct help?"

Lange, still sounding a little sullen, said, "He did. He said he has enough warrior-gender Chelki to man all the small ships we've got, if we need them, and technicians familiar with them to come along. He said he himself intends to go as soon as you tell him where."

John said hastily, "In that dispatch, tell whoever's left on Akiel to bring him." He put the small Hohdan ship in motion toward *Bertha*. The gap closed in less than a minute. They edged in through one of the big hatches. While they waited impatiently for the hatch cover to close and seal and for the bay to pressurize, Vez asked with some anxiety, "John Braysen, where is this world the Vuls are watching?"

John grinned mirthlessly. "Not in the Vulmot Empire. It's in your own region—only a few *doleks'* null from the planet you gave us."

Vez sighed. "Ah. So we had this Klee ship within our reach all the time, had we known it. Well, comrade-in-intrigue, this simplifies things for me, though it prods me deeper into the mire of near-disloyalty. I will do this, if you wish: bring my elite personal guard—thirty ships, all told, though none is above light-cruiser tonnage—and rendezvous wherever you direct. I cannot, in view of recent directives, treat those Vulmoti skulking in our region as pirates. But I can give them every opportunity to make one overt act, and clobber them if they do!"

John tried to think clearly. "Why don't you send a drone, giving coordinates? I'll list them for you." He proceeded to do so.

Vez grinned and turned to his keyboard. "Splendid!"

A light on the console indicated that pressure outside the small ship was now equalized. John opened the lock and they climbed out. He started toward the hatch leading from the bay to a passageway of the immense ship, then paused. "Vez, if we fight a battle around that planet, we might hit the Omniarch."

Vez made the fist-open gesture of agreement. "It is not a planet hospitable to protein life?"

"Very marginally. Dry and poor in oxygen."

Vez pondered for a moment. "Well, I think you had better command, since you've been there before. And it is your species in the balance."

Luna flashed through null. John and Vez sat tense in the two pilots' seats. Both would have preferred emphatically to be aboard *Bertha*, whose marvelous senses could show them the Vul task force ahead of time, but neither wanted to show *Bertha* to Vez Do Han's elite squadron. That would have ended their personal pact right there.

John perspired. How would he handle the situation around the dry planet? He hardly expected the Vul force there to fight; what he expected was that as soon as he broke out of null, they'd run. They must know by now that ships of their own design and construction were aligned with the rebellious Chelki. But what would the long-range effect be of seeing those stolen ships in company with Hohdan fighting vessels? He glanced at Vez. If Vez weren't worried, perhaps John shouldn't be.

But—another thing—where on the arid planet was the Omniarch? Not near that gaping hole from which *Bertha* had risen. That would be deliberate suicide—the Vuls must have looked the hole over thoroughly by now.

And if they guessed that a Klee ship had lain there— well, things would certainly be boiling. They must know about such a ship by now: their spy contacts were as good as Hohd's, and Vez had made the deduction.

If it took him long to pinpoint the Omniarch's hiding place, whole Vul fleets could break out of null around the planet. Certainly Vulmot would risk all-out war with Hohd if the stakes were Klee technology. And John could remember that Vulmot didn't make war dilatorily. He could remember, as if it were the day before yesterday, that moment of utter despair when, suddenly, space around the Terran Fleet was full of blips. He remembered the desperate, stubborn hopelessness with which the Fleet died. Only his instant seizure of a tiniest chance—a chance to merge, for an eternity of two and a fraction minutes, with enemy flotillas, confusing them so that he had time to recharge, launch one complete salvo, and null—had allowed even his wing to escape.

That was almost forty-eight hours after the Destruction of Earth; and still the Vuls had been stalking the Terran Fleet. They could be equally ruthless here.

But, at least, Bart and a few men were safe on *Bertha*. Safe—without the utterly indispensable information the Omniarch carried.

John glanced at the Full Male from Akiel, standing with four feet planted firmly, big hairy hands knotted into fists resting on the forepart of the barrel-shaped body, neck (turretlike) stiffly erect, eyes fixed unblinkingly on the chronometer.

John perspired and watched the same chronometer.

Breakout.

John's mind instantly expelled the various doubts and worries. His eyes darted from dial to screen to mass detector. *There* was a ship of some kind; and *there* . . . Not his own Armed Scouts, nor any of Vez Do Han's ships —they wouldn't be here for ten seconds, to give him time to spot the enemy. Vez, not familiar enough with this ship to program any fighting, was instead busy watching and analyzing enemy forces. "John, that one's within telescopic range! They'll recognize this class of ship!"

John found time to make the fist-open gesture. Then both hands began to move calmly over the keyboard, programming the first data and orders for the rest of the his and Vez's force, when it should arrive. Orders were certainly flashing already between the Vul ships. So far, on this side of the planet, he'd located eleven. All small. . . . From the intercom came Fred Coulter's voice, and Luis Damiano's, and Ralph Cole's. "Telescope contact with one Vul light cruiser. She'll carry twenty heavy missiles, twice as many light ones, four laser clusters and four rupters. . . . She's barely above atmosphere. . . . Command ship probably somewhere beyond the planet. . . . No radio intercepts—they're using beams, of course. . . . No landed ships visible so far. . . ."

Two more blips, then a third, appeared on the radar screens, coming around the curve of the planet to join up with the light cruiser: The third was a big blip—probably a command ship and possibly a *nave* class, like *Luna*. . . .

Then the mass-detector globe was suddenly flecked with blips. John watched them anxiously for a minute, then relaxed a little. They were his own forces.

And, within seconds, all the blips representing Vul forces were gone.

John hit the intercom switch. "All units—search pattern being fed into your computers. Use all the sensors you've got, and your eyes too. We don't know what we're looking for, or listening for, but don't miss anything!"

The blips began shifting about as his own little flotilla and Vez Do Han's elite forces began englobing the planet. John called *Luna*'s Communications Room. "Damiano?"

"Yes, sir."

"Send a drone to Bart Lange every five minutes, with data as we accumulate them."

"Right, Commodore."

John sighed. Now would begin the anxious, blind, sitting-duck phase. The Vuls, of course, still didn't know that the Omniarch was here, but they undoubtedly surmised that this arid world was worth fighting for. How long would it take for some commander to make a decision? Where was the closest authority that could? At some rendezvous in dark space, less than five minutes' null time away? Or hours away, in the Vul region? And how long would this search pattern take to find the Omniarch—if it ever found him?

But he'd underestimated the Omniarch. Barely time enough elapsed for the ships to encircle the planet, and for a few radio messages in English and Hohdan to flash between ships, when a man's voice said tensely, "Number Eight. A flash—looks like a beacon flare—about thirty miles from me. I'm in daylight, but near the evening line. It went off about six or seven thousand feet above the surface."

Simultaneously a pair of Vez's ships were reporting the same flare.

John snapped in English, "Get on it, Number Eight—but be careful!" Then he repeated the order, a bit more courteously, in Hohdan.

And, within minutes, Number Eight said excitedly, "I have a weak radio beam from the ground! It's in English —and I think it's him!"

John, pulse quick with elation, grinned. At a time like this—to hell with grammar!

John, Bart, Vez, the Omniarch, and the Full Male from Akiel sat (or, in the latter two cases, stood) in *Bertha*'s big control room.

The Omniarch seemed unruffled by his narrow escape. "I had oxygen cylinders for ten or twelve hours more, if I didn't gallop about using it too fast." He was speaking in Hohdan. "There was no problem about hiding; I simply hollowed out a hole in the wall of a dry waterway and stayed there. I had my two-way radio, a few biscuits, and a —what is the word? Anyway, a container of water; a 'canteen,' in English. Also, I had that Klee artifact, a remote-control device, that you have all seen now and that John Braysen has seen before. There has been time lately for me to unravel a few more bits of the ancient technology. Since I read the Klee script fairly well now, I was able to summon from its resting place a flare and cause it to detonate. Had you not seen the first, I could have set off another." The four-legged being bent his gaze upon Vez Do Han. "I had not expected the welcome presence of the eminent Field Commander of Integrated Hohdan Home Fleets, with a tidy small force of his own."

Vez had listened expressionlessly to the Omniarch's story, only his eyes showing the turmoil inside him. Now he asked the Chelki levelly in Hohdan, "Is there, then, a large number of Klee artifacts to be claimed from that planet?"

The Omniarch made the little head waggle that indicated

amusement. "There are, indeed, friend and sometimes-ally. So far I have cataloged two hundred and fourteen additional ones." He glanced at John, then back at Vez. "I wonder if you two would care to inform me as to what agreement you have reached. I presume there is one, since you are aboard together."

Vez made the fist-open gesture. "There is. John Braysen has agreed to surrender this ship to me after I help him settle his men and a certain group of human females on some distant planet. I am risking much, for a tremendous stake."

The Omniarch agreed. "So you are—especially if, as I infer from your choice of pronoun, you do not yet have the backing of your empire. Forgive me if I presume to bargain further with you. My own plans have reached a crisis—parts of them have miscarried, though not in a totally unpredictable way. Certain risks have become reality, and I have therefore set in motion contingency actions. My entire species is now in revolt against the Vulmot Empire. I bear upon my spirit the terrible certainty that a great many of us will die. Some will fight their way to temporary freedom and rally at a place from which—if I have interpreted certain things correctly—we may reach ultimate safety. I am talking about numbers in the hundreds of millions." He shifted his feet about. "The escape will depend in part upon a vast ferrying operation already under way and in part upon an escort by fighting vessels. Both of these, and particularly the latter, desperately need assistance, and this I ask of you jointly, John Braysen and Vez Do Han."

John was aware of Vez's gaze, as fixedly as his own upon the Omniarch. There was passion in the Hohdan's voice, and perhaps even a little vituperation. "Just why, ancient one, should I help you? It is not my species that struggles, perhaps hopelessly, for its freedom. If I am engaged at this moment in a certain bit of deviousness, do not interpret that as disloyalty to Hohd! You ask me to risk crews and ships and even our official and largely authentic peace with

Vulmot. What would we gain by incurring those additional risks?"

The Omniarch said calmly, "First of all, you have made a bargain with John Braysen. I did not plan it so, but it fits inextricably into my own problem. Secondly, there are the items to be claimed—as you so accurately state it—from that arid planet within your own regions. Further, there is an additional tremendous depository of Klee artifacts and technology to which I can lead you; and that depository, also, is inseparably welded to my difficulties. It is also in some danger of falling into Vulmotean hands." He smiled a grim, thin-lipped smile and looked at John. "I had better describe this depository by a more significant word. I call it a Vivarium. In it are a number of animal species put there at some time in the past by the Klee; and there, also, are the females of your species, John Braysen." He looked at Vez again. "To reach and take possession of that Vivarium, Vez Do Han, you need my help. The best of your scientists could not reach it in many of your life spans." He paused. "Forgive me—I must correct an inaccuracy in my remark. I do not offer the Vivarium—that I must keep, for it will bear the survivors of my species to safety, or hoped-for safety. The vast number of artifacts stored in it, along with all I know of the technology, I do offer to Hohd."

Vez fairly jumped to his feet, turned his back, and took a dozen agitated steps. Then he whirled and almost ran back to stand facing the big Chelki. "You speak as if the Hohdan Empire could not even contrive to dig up a few buried baubles from a planet in its own region! It sounds to me, four-legged schemer, as if you have run out of all bargaining assets except sheer bluff!"

The Omniarch looked grimly amused. "Try, if you wish. But while you and whatever scientists, technicians, and excavating engineers you may summon dig with utter futility into the crust of this planet, the Vuls will be pursuing equally determined plans. Nor will they—nor the Bizh— have failed to reach conclusions about this monstrous ship we are aboard. Without me, and without the cooperation of other Chelki much closer to the greedy grasp of Vulmot than to yours, you are likely to come third in the race."

Vez snarled, "Who owns this ship—this *Bertha,* whatever that means—at this moment?"

The Omniarch said with grim amusement, "John Braysen owns and commands it at this moment. But he is under contract to me, and that contract is secured by something of the utmost importance to him. As to any liens he may have given you upon the ship—those are his decision and do not interest me beyond the temporary employment of the ship."

Vez again turned his back on the Chelki and asked of John tersely, "Will you provide me with a few dispatch drones? If I am to plunge full depth into this madness, I must assemble a larger force. And to do that I must speak of Klee artifacts."

John didn't hesitate. He wanted this haggling to be ended. "Certainly, comrade-in-arms."

(20)

Luna MOVED swiftly above the surface of the arid planet. John nervously watched the mass detector. Vez sat in the second pilot's seat, ready to send hasty dispatch drones to his augmented forces lurking a few null-seconds away. The Omniarch squatted beside the Klee remote-control device.

No intruders had appeared so far.

The Omniarch called, "I have something, Vez Do Han. Let us not go any closer, John Braysen."

John stopped the ship and hovered. They were a mile above the surface. The Omniarch made finer adjustments, then pressed some studⁿ

For a moment ┉ing happened. Then Luna's klaxon began to bleat. Jc ┉ shot looks at instruments. This was a routine enough alarm: some considerable, but not immense, mass of metal had come within close range. Nervously he turned off the klaxon. Then he saw, on a side viewer, dirt and rocks boiling up. He punched keys for a magnified view.

Something rose slowly into sight, as the huge Klee ship had risen when he first saw it. This was much smaller —no more than two hundred feet long, and possibly forty in diameter. The surface was medium gray, without projections or other features. The shape was a perfect cylinder. He calculated mentally. To have set off the alarm, this thing must be quite dense—no mere thin-walled tank would have done it. He watched it rise slowly. "Is it safe to take aboard, Omniarch?"

"It is, John Braysen; but first let me demonstrate something!" He bent over the control device again.

In the viewer John saw a tiny object appear just below the now hovering cylinder and fall to the ground. Vez Do Han asked doubtfully, "A hatch? A bomb bay?"

"Neither," the Omniarch said. "The small thing that fell was a unit package of fuel wire. I ordered the canister to null the package outside itself. You could not extract it in any other way, short of destruction of the canister. The canister itself is, shall I say, a delivery device. It is full of unit packages of fuel wire—nothing else, except its own machinery. But that machinery, Vez Do Han, will fascinate and baffle your scientists for several generations, even with the hints I can give them."

John said nervously, "I can just get the thing into Number Four Hatch and Hold. If we had *Bertha* here . . ." He shrugged mentally and opened the hatch. The Omniarch tediously brought the canister to them and into *Luna*'s biggest opening.

Eleven hours passed. At the end of that time *Bertha was* there—they'd had to summon her to take aboard all the artifacts. The dry soil had disgorged four more fuel-wire canisters, twenty-odd smaller delivery devices containing (the Omniarch said) chemicals, stocks of metal bars and sheets, tools, instruments, and even food in sealed packages. That last, both Vez and John insisted on seeing—and did. The stuff (mostly a sort of field ration not unlike pemmican) came from the rather simple metal containers in perfect condition.

Perhaps it was that latter that set both Vez and John thinking. It was Vez (as *Bertha* flashed through null to unload the booty in a place Vez decided was safe) who first voiced the mind-numbing thoughts. "Omniarch, as I go over earlier dialogue, it strikes me that you have never actually said that Klee items were *buried in this planet*."

The big Chelki looked amused. "That is correct, Vez Do Han."

"And," Vez went on, "all of them appeared very suddenly on the mass detector. Had they been buried—even a mile deep—they would have shown when we approached.

Therefore, they were *not* here. You summoned each of them from somewhere else!"

"Entirely correct. Here were only markers of a sort."

Vez laughed. "So you did not lie when you said I could dig all I wished. All right—I deceived myself, if anyone did. Now, where is the depot from which you summoned them? Far distant, no doubt. And what can one deduce, except that Klee, or users of Klee technology, still occupy and operate that depot?" He walked over, very serious now, and faced the Chelki. "You cannot ask me to believe that food—even the most marvelously preserved food—has lasted *thirty thousand years!*"

"I will not ask you to believe that, Vez Do Han, although I would not be surprised if it *could* be so." He paused. "What I am going to tell you may be even less credible. The physical distance from which I brought the items is something I cannot evaluate—nor does it matter. What does matter is that I brought them a nonphysical distance of *thirty thousand years.*"

Both John and Vez stared at him until he smiled. "Do not take it so hard, friends and allies. The fact, as I perhaps inaccurately see it, is that the Klee had partially conquered time. They could not travel into the past—*their* past, I should call it. But they could hold an object, even a very large one, motionless in time. At least, for short periods. And they could project objects forward in time —though, I think, they had not completed the study of that phenomenon when something overtook them or diverted them." He paused, giving them time to breathe. "They set up depots, with appropriate machinery, to project supplies —caches, if you will—far forward ahead of themselves. By a roundabout route, I stumbled across a few—planted instructions, shall we say?—and at least two unmanned probes into their far future. Into nearly *our* time. The more ambitious of the two, I call the Vivarium. It is immense—it dwarfs this ship. In it, John Braysen, are the women. And in it, Vez Do Han, is the great depository of Klee artifacts I promised you." He paused. "These items I summoned up via the arid planet are from somewhere else—some depot, set up to supply an expedition they intended to send after the Vivarium. We must presume that such an expedition was never sent, or met with disaster, since it has left no signs of itself and has not drawn upon this 'cache.' Though perhaps there were other caches." He smiled his thin-lipped smile. "Somewhere, friends—I should say *some-when*'—a depot is faithfully operating, dispatching through the millenia supplies for that expedition. Perhaps Klee are still alive; perhaps, by calling up these supplies, we have caused the greatest excitement among them. If so, they cannot be sure that it *is* their expedition summoning the cache. They may be reconciled to its use by aliens far in their future. They can never know. Only their extremely remote descendants could know. And there seem to be none."

John found his voice first. "This—this Vivarium. You say the women are in it. And that the Vuls are looking for it."

"Yes, John Braysen, but they cannot find it unless they capture me and all my knowledge. For it is not in their 'present.' I have visited it twice, and the latter time, I sent it—'held' it, is more accurate—into their, and our, 'past.' The terms are not at all accurate—the two are separated by far more than the mere elapsed time. It is as if they were parallel but separated planes, perpendicular to a straight line—which we call time—and moving along it, one after the other."

Vez asked incredibly, "You *held* it back in time?"

"Yes. As I told you, *that* is possible."

John, pulse quickening with anger, glared at the Chelki. "You mean to say the women are *unreachable*?"

"Unreachable from our 'present,' yes. They are quite safe, so long as they stay there, from the Vulmoti. But I can—and must, since my own species needs the Vivarium —bring your women, and the whole Vivarium, into our 'present.'"

More gaping. And then Vez asked very doubtingly,

"You say you held the Vivarium back. If I understand what you mean, how did you get back into our 'present'? Or should I say *forward* into our present?"

The Chelki made the sound that corresponded to a chuckle. "Do not sprain your mind, Vez Do Han, upon the paradoxes of the situation. My return was quite simple, though I grant I waited nervously. I already had this gadget." He nudged the control device. "I left it here—in our 'present,' I mean. And I had it set to summon back, or forward, the small ship I used for the trip. It performed —and I am here."

After a dazed silence John asked slowly, "Just how far in the past *are* the women? And the Vivarium?"

The Omniarch's dark, deep-set eyes glittered. "About six *doleks*. That is, about thirteen and a quarter minutes. But they might as well be in another galaxy."

Vez Do Han spent some time in *Bertha*'s Communications Room, sending off dispatch drones and impatiently awaiting replies. When he returned to Main Control he was grinning widely. "My superiors, and civilians of the government, have had a hasty look at the Klee artifacts from that arid planet, and the situation has altered drastically. We still, of course, want to avoid all-out war with Vulmot. But I am authorized to go to almost any length to take possession of the additional artifacts I promised. Not only may I take my elite guard anywhere, but also my superiors are throwing in almost the entire catalog of alien-built ships we have acquired during recent history. Two capital ships comparable to *Luna*. Thirty-odd cruisers, nearly half of them Heavies. And a hundred, more or less, of miscellaneous smaller ships, all armed. The larger ships will bring loads of munitions and supplies for any smaller vessels that may be short of them—missiles, fuel wire, food!" He looked at the Omniarch. "The understanding is, of course, that I am to bring back all additional artifacts I find. I did not mention what you call a Vivarium."

The big Chelki said impatiently, "We have already

agreed upon that. When will these additional forces be here?"

"Within fifty or sixty *doleks*. As soon as they can toss aboard what they are bringing."

The Omniarch shuffled his feet about and scowled. "I must suggest, then, that we go on ahead, leaving a dispatch ship here to direct them after us. We cannot wait."

Vez looked unwilling. "We will be twenty *doleks* getting ready to leave, ourselves! And we need those munitions!"

The Omniarch made a sound like a low growl. "If we must, we can arrange a rendezvous short of the one I'd planned. But I insist on starting as soon as possible. My people can dodge about a bit to avoid trouble, and we can still find them. But we *must* be near!"

Vez sighed. "All right—where shall we rendezvous?"

The Omniarch spieled off coordinates. John recognized them as being far out along the Sparse Regions between spiral arms—almost as far as he'd gone to do a little mapping for Vez, at the far end of the Bizh Empire. Vez left to send messages and more drones.

While he was gone, the Omniarch talked. "I do not know the size of the fleet we may find. Slave Chelki on hundreds of worlds were to seize whatever ships they can, armed or not armed, and rendezvous near one spot. Some will be thwarted, and I fear that the Vulmoti uncovered the plan soon enough to message many worlds and forestall it entirely. Millions of Chelki will die in the attempt, and millions more will be herded into makeshift prison camps. The search for those who escape will be immediate and furious." He turned his dark eyes to John. "You have observed the utter ruthlessness of the Vulmoti, John Braysen, when they have made a decision. They decided that your species must be annihilated. Now they may make the same decision about mine." He brooded awhile, pacing about the Control Room. "We cannot, like your species— or like other humanoids—scatter and live in small groups. That is not a viable way of life even for a Full Male over any length of time. We must have the awareness of a colony about us, or within short traveling time. We must have a sense of continuing past, present, and future. Those needs have complicated our long search for freedom."

It struck John for the first time that humanoids must seem, to the Chelki, a remarkably adaptable species. The meekest humanoid technician—male or female—could, if necessary, seize a weapon and fight. Or fight with bare hands, with tooth and fingernail! He sat watching the Omniarch for a minute. "This—this Vivarium you've been speaking of. As I understand it, there are various living environments in it. But—gods of space! Is it big enough to put *millions* of your people in?"

"It is, John Braysen. And its automatic machinery, including the energy converters, is staggering. I have spent quite a number of hours actually staring at that machinery and made a few infinitesimal experiments with it, and many thousands of hours since, pondering. Yet I have only the faintest comprehension of small bits of it." He stared at John, and his eyes were haunted. "Even the facet with which I hope to take my people to safety is an almost total mystery to me. I have tried to assemble a team of qualified individuals to help me study it, when they and I shall be aboard. I do not know how many of them may reach rendezvous. And even when I have brought the Vivarium out of the past, there will still be the job of getting my people aboard. That will be a huge task."

John was silent for a minute. Then, "Perhaps you don't want to tell me, for security's sake, where you intend to take your people for safety? I assume the Vivarium is capable of nulling." He paused. "You know, I too have the problem of finding some planet far enough from the Vulmoti to be safe." The Omniarch didn't smile as he said, "However long your journey, it will be nothing compared to mine. When the women are out of the Vivarium and my people—those who have been able to escape—are aboard, I hope to take the Vivarium into the far future."

The Full Male from Akiel had walked over to stand beside the Omniarch—like two male bovines, John thought, forming a rank to protect cows and calves behind them. He sat staring at them, his mind a little dazed. Finally he asked numbly, "What will you do if something goes wrong? If you can't operate the machinery as you hope?"

"Then," said the Omniarch, "there will be no freedom for Chelki. I and my descendant here will simply poison ourselves."

(21)

BERTHA SPED through null. John, Bart Lange, and the two male Chelki stood before the spring-mounted instrument panel. In the optical simulation of a transparent sphere, amber blips were loosely grouped about the center. Those represented all the ships accompanying *Bertha*— John's tiny fleet, including *Luna*, Vez Do Han's elite guard, and the additional miscellaneous ships given Vez by his superiors. All of those blips would have been gathered together into a tight knot, were they viewed fifteen minutes earlier, for the ships they represented had clustered together at the first rendezvous, while cargoes were interchanged. Now, armed and provisioned, they were on the way to the second rendezvous.

Bart Lange stepped closer to the panel and turned knobs. The cluster of blips around the center of the sphere shrank together. Far out near the edge of the sphere, a diffuse blob now glowed. Those tiny blips, too small individually and too numerous to count, represented the huge migration of escaped Chelki. Obviously there were more than a few.

Bart looked up suddenly at the Omniarch. "Say—by the way, why is this panel mounted on springs?"

The Omniarch looked absent for a moment. "Oh—those aren't springs. They're insulators." He reached out a hairy big hand and touched one edge of the panel. Immediately, dial needles quivered, lights flickered, and the blips in the nonmaterial sphere danced. "See? By touching the panel, I affected its charge. Not an electrical charge, but something distantly related. The whole panel must be highly charged for its instruments to operate. Hence, insulators—of some special plastic of low density."

Bart looked startled, then frowned. "Why doesn't the charge leak off through the air?"

Even now, the big Chelki was able to smile. "It is not that kind of a charge." He turned his attention back to the false sphere. "We cannot see, from this distance, whether my people have managed to seize armed ships, or whether those are mostly cargo vessels. One thing, though, we shall see, if it happens: if Vulmoti appear, my people will scatter. Then we will have to find them again." He turned his eyes to John. "For safety in breaking out of null, they will occupy a volume of space a million miles across, or more. There'll be stragglers arriving, safely short of the central point, and moving in to join up. How do you propose to escort such a mass of ships?"

John had been pondering that. He'd been visualizing a very large herd of sheep, escorted by only a few shepherds and dogs, in wild country where wolves and coyotes lurked. "Well, I suggest that when we arrive, we get them all moving in a column, on grav drive, toward the target point. That way, any stragglers will still break out within detector range and be able to catch up. We'll put most of our own force, plus whatever fighting ships your people have seized, in the forefront. That way we'll be near any Vul searchers who break out ahead of the column. We'll have pickets scattered along each side of the column."

Bart protested, "If the ships are moving in a column, won't a few stragglers break out right in the front of it?"

John looked at the Omniarch. "I suspect the plan has a built-in provision for that."

"Yes," the ancient Chelki said. "I anticipated that the gathering might have to make short null hops to avoid suddenly appearing Vul searchers. I specified that those hops *not* be along the intended line of travel—but rather, at some distance to the sides of it."

John nodded slowly. "Of course, there's likely to be a

certain amount of confusion. A few simple mistakes. And a few ships that didn't get the messages in the first place."

The Omniarch looked away for a minute. "Undoubtedly. I fear we cannot avoid tragedies. Let us try to minimize them." He looked at the sphere again. "Only a little while more. I find that a mercy; this wait has been intolerable."

Breakout!

John tried to watch both the mass-detector and the data screens at once. Gods of space! Two thousand, two hundred and seventy-odd ships within normal range, and still the count grew steadily! Two thousand and three hundred plus . . . Two thousand and four hundred . . . *Bertha's* detector spheres seemed full of effervescent liquid, as stragglers popped out of null, each contributing one more blip.

The figures on the data screen still mounted. But the rate of increase was slowing. Minutes, quarter-hours, an hour crawled by. And now the figure grew only slowly, until a whole minute went by without an increase. Then one more straggler arrived. Two minutes . . . another straggler . . . three minutes . . . two more blips, simultaneously . . . John, his insides a turmoil, said, "You *must* have set a cutoff time."

The Omniarch's dark eyes rested on him. "We are past it already, of course. The count of ships here is much smaller than I had hoped. I found it hard to say, coldly. Now we shall go."

John threw an anxious glance at the long-range detector. No Vuls had shown yet; or if they had, they'd been buried in the mass of other blips. How would anyone know? All these ships were of Vul design. How many spies might lurk among them? He sighed. "We'll leave a dispatch ship here, of course, to direct any later stragglers after us."

"If you think it safe, John Braysen." The Omniarch was standing four-solid before an intercom outlet, where he could reach a computer keyboard. Already Chelki voices were murmuring over the radio—ships' pilots and commanders, reporting in, giving what information they had. It would be many minutes before any sort of organization could be shaped out of that mass of ships.

John said, "First of all, find out how many fighting ships you have, and what class. Make as sure as you can that you are talking to *Chelki*."

The Omniarch flashed him a tight smile. The Full Male from Akiel moved over near John. "Not to worry about that, Co-mo-dore. Now that we are in—in rebellion as a species, we cannot be forced to lie to an Omniarch. Warriors or Full Males would die fighting, if they had one hand or one foot free. If not, they would poison themselves. Other genders would not—*could* not—be trai-tors either."

John, busy trying to make some sense out of the vast array of ships, nodded doubtfully. Let the Omniarch, then, worry about the problem of spies. He called over to that ancient Chelki, "Choose a picket ship to leave behind."

"I have already chosen, John Braysen—a heavy cruiser, with full radio and sensor equipment. It is already moving to the side. It will send any late stragglers after us." He spoke a few more words of Chelki into the radio, listened for a minute, and looked at John again. "Eleven fighting ships to join you, John Braysen: five heavy cruisers, six medium cruisers. Twenty-three Armed Scouts. Most of them are very short of missiles, as they were aground when seized."

John frowned. Not much help, if a real Vul force caught him. "Bring them in around *Bertha*, in fairly close formation. You can talk to them by weak radio beam without confusing everyone else. I can't feed lock-in programs to their computers, so you'll have to relay orders verbally. And they'll have to pilot themselves." He leaned toward his own intercom pickup grille. "Damiano?"

"Yes, sir."

"Give the Omniarch all the help you can in holding contact with his various Chelki-crewed units."

"Right, sir."

John darted looks around at screens and instruments.

He had a fix now on the ship that was to stay behind. The column in grav drive wasn't adequately formed up yet.

But then, abruptly, there were other blips on a screen. He gave it a quick look. "Null out! Null out!"

Bart had the from-null detector system working and tuned to close range. Sickly, John leaned toward it to watch the small tragedy being shown there. One blip—the ship chosen to stay behind—darted about like a frantic gnat. A dozen and more other blips pursued it, intercepted it, hemmed it in with deadly professionalism. A few more small blips appeared suddenly from time to time—and went into immediate flight on grav drive. Those were stragglers, breaking out, seeing the hopeless fight, and running just as hopelessly.

The fugitive blip vanished. That ship no longer existed as any single mass large enough to show. And now the Vul ships turned to pursuit of the few stragglers. One by one those hapless blips vanished too, as Vul ships, recharged by now, nulled into their paths and blasted them.

One dodging blip did seem to make it—it vanished with no Vul pursuer near it, which probably meant it had lasted long enough to null. But to where? No one remained at the deserted rendezvous point to direct it. The Chelki aboard, whatever their gender, were lost—isolated from their species, like a few ants whose nest has been destroyed.

Time crawled by. The elongated swarm of blips surrounding the center of the mass-detector globe (now switched to in-null operation) had been slowly expanding for some time. That was proper—the vast migration *had* to expand, so individual ships wouldn't break out, at the end, within one another. It must be an agonizing thing, aboard those ships; none of them, like *Bertha,* could see what was around them in null. Each was blind, like any single ship in null.

"John."

He turned at Bart's voice, left his seat, and went over to join the other man before the insulation-mounted panel. The sphere on this panel did not show the migration around them—its blips, when there were any, showed objects in normal space—but, at the edge, a point of familiar blue-violet light had appeared. Very slowly, it moved inward.

"Remember that?" Bart asked.

John remembered it. And he suddenly turned toward the Omniarch, slowly pacing not far away. "Is this where we're going?"

"Yes, John Braysen."

John looked at Bart. "We were right there. *Right* there!"

Bart grinned. "Yes. But we were thirteen minutes too soon."

And now another eternity of waiting began. As nearly as *Bertha*'s sensors and computers could keep track, all of the ships bearing Chelki were keeping pace. Some had diverged far enough to the sides to be isolated individual blips, but the count held steady (except for the small variance up and down as ships were masked one by another). John and Vez joined the Omniarch in pacing.

At one point John asked the Chelki, "How does this detector system register ships so far away, and distinguish them from inert objects?"

"It has something to do with the expenditure of energy. Even a ship at rest has some process or other going on within it—if nothing more than air regeneration and the operation of sensors. If the converters are running, turning fuel wire into stored energy, that registers. Charging for null registers. If a ship is already charged for null, that registers; and a grav drive; and so on. I think, John Braysen, that an absolutely inert ship, with no charge of any sort upon it, would not be registered."

John shrugged and resumed pacing.

More time dragged, but the chronometer needle was stuttering toward the mark. A time arrived when everyone in the Control Room held his breath, watching. The needle made a few more tiny jumps, and . . .

Breakout!

The screens were almost solid with blips. The radio came alive—English, Hohdan, Chelki. The klaxon bleated; John stared at instruments, made sure the too close ship wasn't going to ram them, and turned the klaxon off. The Omniarch, after some hasty radio talk, looked at John and said, "Two ships broke out partly overlapping, I think— there was a complete disintegration, and they are gone, though a ghost image of finely divided matter shows in the vicinity. One of the light cruisers reports that its fire-control circuits are out of order."

John said hastily, "Have it move away from the rest of us, in case missiles launch by malfunction."

"I have done that, John Braysen."

Again, that hopeless chaos—this time as ships, cautiously separated for the null trip, now converged again on gravs. John let the computers struggle to keep track of them, and watched the mass-detector system anxiously. The Vuls might have captured some Chelki alive, but unconscious, and somehow dragged from him the location of this new rendezvous. He looked at a screen that showed the outer spiral arm. He could imagine fleets, with implacable purpose, flashing through null from that direction.

The Omniarch placed the control device on the deck, face up, and knelt to turn knobs gingerly. John felt like screaming, "Hurry! Hurry!" He saw the Omniarch pause and draw a deep breath that swelled out his barrel-shaped body. And—the big hairy hands were trembling.

Hurry!

It seemed hours that the big old Chelki knelt there, four legs doubled awkwardly beneath him, hands fumbling slowly at knobs, dark deep-set eyes peering down at the device. Then the big being pushed a stud, sighed, and climbed slowly to his feet. John shot a glance at the chronometer. Seventeen minutes had crawled by while the Omniarch was at work.

"How long now?" Bart Lange exploded.

The dark eyes turned toward him. "Two minutes, perhaps."

John waited, looked at the chronometer, waited again, and once more looked at the chronometer. It didn't seem possible that the needle could crawl around so slowly. A minute . . . fifty seconds . . . Unable to bear just waiting, he uncoiled from his seat and strode to the insulator-mounted panel. Nothing there, of course: they weren't in null. Space, he was dizzy! He crossed over to the normal-space device. It, of course, was full of blips. What did he expect?

Compulsively, his eyes went to the chronometer. *Four seconds! Three . . . Two . . .*

The needle reached the mark and passed on. Another second; two, three. Nothing happened. John's stomach, already knotted, twinged as if something had broken. *Something had failed!*

And then, suddenly, soundlessly, with no forewarning, the whole Control Room—deck, bulkheads, overhead, every instrument and switch and knob, every living occupant—*everything* was covered with, bathed in, a purplish-blue luminescence.

John gasped. The thought knifed through his mind that this might be some deadly radiation—that in one instant he might feel an awful burning, a stab of pain, a knotting of muscles until they tore. He felt nothing, unless that agonized tightness of his midriff could be counted. But that was familiar—he knew it of old. It was fear.

Vez was snarling something. And the Omniarch's calm voice replied, "Just an energy spill. Everything within a million miles, I do not doubt, is aglow with it. Watch the forward screens!"

And even as he spoke, something was forming on those screens. An outline—no, it quickly grew solid! John drew a painful ragged breath. Vaguely, he heard someone—Ralph Cole, he thought—shouting over the radio. He walked limply, eyes still on the screens, to his seat and squirmed into it. "All right, Cole—what are you yelling about?"

"Commodore! It's almost two hundred miles long, and fifty in diameter! But the mass detectors—"

Belatedly, the klaxon bleated. John reached out limply and turned it off. The actual, material mass of that thing must have been slow to—to materialize in . . . He shook his head dazedly. In this "present," the Omniarch called it.

But now it was here, and the sensors all reported it. He punched shakily for data and watched them scroll across the screen. No need to quibble. Ralph Cole had been near enough right the first time.

He was aware of the Omniarch spieling crisp Chelki into the radio. A minute later the big four-legged creature pointed a hairy finger at a screen. John saw a single blip darting toward the colossal cylinder that loomed in space, seemingly so close. He had wits enough to shout into his own intercom, "Cole! Get a telescope on that Chelki ship!"

Everyone was silent now. But minutes later Ralph Cole reported, "Commodore, a hole must have opened in the end of tl. ...ng and taken the ship inside!"

Vez Do Han completed another impatient stroll .oss the Control Room, turned, and came back to face the Omniarch. "I share, of course, your anxiety about your own people. Also John's concern for the human females. However, my duty here involves the Klee artifacts you promised me. When, and how, will we consummate that promise?"

The Omniarch found time to look amused. "As soon as the first scout ship emerges and reports that there are no problems, shiploads of my people will begin to enter. You can understand that distribution will take some time and that there will be a certain amount of traffic congestion even inside that large cylinder—especially since ingress and egress are through a central hub. But as soon as we start entering, there will be no reason why you should not send ships inside and begin removing artifacts. And at the same time, of course, John Braysen can begin ferrying out

THERE WAS a long passageway, none too roomy for the small ship, with various side locks which must lead into the space between the inner and outer shafts. Then another airlock, and they emerged into the living segment.

It was not until they'd moved a few miles away from the hub that John could see the whole enormous segment in its proper perspective.

The two flat walls, immense disks of metal, were thirty-plus miles apart. The hub, running between the centers of the two walls, was like a long tube (if something a half-mile or more thick could be called a "tube"). Only the very short fraction of it at one end, whence they'd emerged, was dark all the way around. For the rest of the thirty miles, one side of the "tube" was blindingly radiant. That was the "sun." The side unlit at this moment permitted a sort of "night."

The "land" covered the entire circular wall of what was simply an immense flat cylinder eighty-odd miles across, with the hub running along its axis. It covered that curve from one flat "end" to the other, and all around the vast circle. Against the ends, it was piled up in mountains. In the middle were the lowlands—and an "ocean" into which rivers drained, and which stretched continuously, though not with constant width, clear around the cylinder's curved wall. Meadows bordered that ocean. Between the meadows and the foothills, brushland and forest were intermingled. The grass was a normal enough shade of green, and so were some of the trees; but other trees, and most of the brush, were various hues of yellow or orange.

Wasn't that snow topping the highest peaks along the nearer wall? It certainly was! So the "hub" provided seasons, as well as day and night.

His pulse was a thunder in his temples now. He let the ship speed laterally and around the great curve of land. They were down to within ten miles of the land now, and instruments were registering the artificial gravity. He punched hasty calculations on the computer. They said that at ground level the gravity would be close to one gee. With clumsy hands he directed the ship's telescope toward the spot where (the Omniarch claimed) the women and girl children had been set down nearly ten years ago.

He saw nothing. Of course, he told himself, they could have migrated far around the curve by now.

He glanced at other viewscreens. This far from the hub, he could see most of the opposite curve of land. There was no essential difference from this one.

Fred Coulter came to stand beside him. "There was supposed to be a creek. And a grove of trees just where the creek ran onto the meadow."

" ve got the place pinpointed," John said tersely. The anxiety was a pain in his lungs and his stomach, a trembling of every muscle. He strained his eyes at the magnified view of the spot. Nothing; and "day" was beginning to fade here. Lower . . .

Fred Coulter grabbed his shoulder. "There! A—a tepee!"

John saw it. And his hands could hardly program the ship down.

His compact pistol dangling from his hand—in case there were dangerous beasts prowling the vicinity—John walked across the meadow. The grass smelled like Earth grass, but the clumpy bushes along the creek were an odd saffron color. A strange tinkling noise seemed to come from those bushes. Fred Coulter, at his shoulder, muttered something. Several yards behind them were all but one of the other men.

They reached the edge of the grove of trees and

stopped, peering at the collection of huts and tents a few yards into the shade. The place seemed deserted. John's nerves twinged harder. He swallowed hard. Space; for a little *dron* . . . He took a deep breath and tried to call out, "Hello?" Only a feeble sound emerged. The second try was better. "HELLO!"

From somewhere fifty yards or so into the thicket came a muffled scream. Then a single, frightened, soprano call, "Hello?"

Suddenly he and the other men were shouting, weeping, running, stumbling into one another. John dropped his pistol somewhere. The screaming and crying of many feminine voices made a clamor just beyond a screen of trees. They were coming this way.

The first woman burst into sight. . . .

And, abruptly, strangely, all the noise was gone. Two groups stood utterly still, staring at each other. John's chest ached so that he wondered if he were having a heart attack.

Then from somewhere in the group of women came a small, incredulous, desperately hopeful voice. *"Fred?"*

Coulter let out his breath in a sob, drew it in again, almost strangling on it. *"Eloise?"* he choked out unbelievingly.

The woman clawed and shoved her way out of the crowd. Fred made an incoherent sound and ran to meet her. They collided; nearly fell; grabbed at each other and managed to keep their feet, hugging each other as hard as they could, babbling meaningless sounds.

Everyone just stood watching for a moment. No other woman, not one of the men, moved. But suddenly everyone in both groups was racked with uncontrollable sobs.

(23)

Ferrying the women out took four hours. During most of it, John stayed at *Bertha*'s control console, anxiously watching for blips that might be Vul scouts breaking out of null. There were plenty of telltale blips on the long-range detectors, and they told of a mighty search pattern. One way or another, the Vuls had narrowed things down to this general region of space.

But on the last ferrying trip—a superfluous one, perhaps, to pick up a few personal belongings left behind by the women—John went himself, taking four men and the rather young woman named Lisa Duval who was currently "First" of the pathetic little feminine colony. She was a girl of medium height, lithe, with Latin skin and features, who said little but whose dark eyes took in everything. They moved through the long central shaft and into the segment.

When they'd found the few missing items—a rag doll, an old pitted mirror that had come from Earth, a few worn garments—Lisa paused, looking around the deserted camp. There was moisture in her eyes. John realized that here she'd grown from childhood to young womanhood. It wasn't surprising that she was just a little sad at leaving forever.

Then suddenly she turned on him with a hint of defiance in her eye. "I know we shouldn't delay, but there's some-one I must say good-bye to!"

He gaped at her. "You mean—one of you's been hiding, unwilling to go? And you didn't tell us?"

She shook her head vigorously. "Not a human. Come

176

along, if you like." She met his look squarely.

He knew he must be scowling. "Well, let's hurry it up!"

They followed a trail that led up the creek past a big clump of the saffron-colored bushes ("tinklebushes"; well named) into a grove of trees like Terran poplars, as he remembered them, around the base of a low hill, to the very edge of the creek.

A fat, gray-furred creature that must weigh over fifty pounds suddenly moved toward them from beside a burrow opening. He got the impression that it must have been sitting there staring down the path. He glanced in surprise at the hillside. There were odd little structures—it seemed that the hill was honeycombed with burrows and that most of the entrances had little shacklike shelters, of interwoven twigs and branches, over them.

Now that he saw it closer, the animal made John think of a very large, very fat beaver. He put a hand nervously to his pistol pocket as it waddled urgently toward them. It had big, strong, chisel-shaped teeth. . . .

He let out his breath in a sigh of relief and surprise as it spoke in understandable English. "Lee-sa! I was afraid you not come, say good-bye!"

Lisa went forward, all soft girlishness, and dropped to her knees. The creature squatted on its haunches, seeming to become a ball of fur, and extended a paw. Lisa touched the paw, as if in ritual. "I couldn't," she said. "Though we are in a terrible hurry, and I cannot stay long."

The creature actually shed two round tears. "Miss you we, Tall Furless One, Tall Good Neighbor."

Lisa seemed to be crying a little too. "We shall miss you too, Good Neighbors. Will you say good-bye for me to your husband, and to your two brave sons, and all of the clan?"

"Do that I, Tall Neighbor. So happy we, your males have come." The fat creature turned a moist pair of eyes on John. "Go you all away now, forever?"

"We must, Gentle Neighbor. We shall never forget all the favors you have done us. And we shall wish the wish of Good Fortune for you every night and morning."

The fat creature squirmed a little. "You were best neighbors, too—you guarded us from the Large Beasts." It sighed. "What do we now? Husband mine try make weapons, like you had. But our hands—our paws—not right."

Lisa said, "There are other beings—strong, wise ones —coming into the place now. They will not let the Large Beasts harm you."

The creature looked doubtful. "They big? They have meat fangs, eat us?"

Lisa turned a troubled look to John. He said gruffly, "The Chelki are civilized. And they're vegetarian."

Lisa got slowly to her feet. "We must go now, old friend and generous neighbor."

The beast stared up at her and produced two more tears. Good-bye. Please—call I you by secret name? Husband mine say, silly, because you not our kind."

Lisa said muffledly, "Of course you may."

The creature said, "Good-bye, Fairest of the Clan."

Lisa was crying quietly as they hurried away. John looked back once. The fat creature still squatted there, staring after them sadly.

The situation that developed immediately aboard *Bertha* was unexpected and surprising. John couldn't explain it logically, but he *felt*, along with the others, that it was right. Vez and his handful of Hohdan specialists, now part of *Bertha*'s complement, tended to grin about it.

Fred and Eloise Coulter had a living compartment to themselves. All the other men, though, and all the women, somehow shrank from the notion of pairing off and setting up housekeeping. The women wanted to continue living together as a group—in their own section of *Bertha*—and the men felt the same. Not that there weren't clandestine liaisons (a few of which, embarrassingly interrupted, became shipwide jokes), but the overall attitude was one of reverence between the sexes. Maybe it existed because both groups had lived celibate so long. Or maybe it was some deeper sense of responsibility, some fierce dedication to the future of the species.

At any rate, there were almost no problems of competition, even though the men outnumbered the women by nearly two to one.

The Chelki ingress into the Vivarium was almost complete. Still the Vul search pattern had not scored its inevitable bull's-eye. John and Vez Do Han spent much of their time pacing the big Control Room impatiently. When they occasionally met face to face, each would scowl and reverse course.

Finally Vez broke this pattern. He planted his feet firmly and stared John in the eye. "Comrade, there is an item we must discuss."

John sighed and stopped pacing. "You mean, how long are we going to stay here gua ، ، the Vivarium after the Chelki are all settled in?"

"Precisely. You have your females, and I have most of the artifacts I can haul. Our agreement with each other is definite. Our agreement with the Omniarch is vague. Must we defer our own affairs indefinitely while he putters around about his study of the Vivarium's machinery?"

John swallowed. The *dron* thirst was a constant distress. "I hope not indefinitely! But our bargain with him implies at least a short period of grace for him to work in."

Vez looked impatient. "Yes, yes. But how long would you say a short period should be?"

John said, "I don't know. But I'm not willing to put the prod to him right now—when I know he's not even taking time to eat or sleep!"

Vez made an annoyed fist-open gesture of agreement. "Do not put me in the position of hangman! I am not suggesting we null away ten *doleks* from now. But how long is long enough?"

John pushed down his own impatience. "Do not put me in the position of answer machine, with everything programmed in! I will tell you what—though I hate to waste his time, I'm going to radio him right now and put the question to him!"

Vez scowled as if he didn't like that answer, either.

There was no video hookup with the inside of the Vivarium, so they couldn't see the Omniarch's face, but his voice was very tired. "I can understand your impatience. But I can offer no salve for it. There are encouraging results here, but not yet adequate ones. The situation is this: I am almost sure I can operate the time-leap machinery now. However, we have found damage in various parts of the Vivarium—not damage from space debris, but something that went wrong internally, a long time ago. I did not find it when I was here before. There is even a hole in the wall between the segment where your females were and the next—possibly they can describe it to you. I do not know whether other damage, closer to the machinery, will affect a time-leap. You will recall that so far I have held back, and later advanced, the Vivarium a matter of only a few minutes. This time I must take it many thousands of years—only thus can I hope that the Vuls will have forgotten their rage." The voice hesitated wearily. "We are working very hard, trying to trace all the damage and analyze, if we can, its effect on the machinery. I ask this of you: give me at the very least ten more hours. Will you do that?"

John glanced at Vez. Vez irritably made the fist-opening gesture. John told the Omniarch, "We will. And good luck."

The watch for enemy blips resumed. The Vul search pattern, as seen by *Bertha*'s long-range senses, didn't appear to be coming any closer. Two hours went by, then another. John began to hope that, for some reason, the Vuls were rejecting this precise part of space.

And then the klaxon suddenly began bleating.

John jerked a glance at the mass-detector globe. Gods of space! The region around the center was a mass of strong blips! He darted a look at data screens. *One thousand and four hundred plus . . . One thousand and six hundred plus . . .* Never, except for the vast gathering of fugitive Chelki in seized ships, had he seen a fraction of a fleet like this. And these were all fighting ships! He punched studs, stared briefly at screens, punched other studs. Voices were shouting on the intercom now, in English and Hohdan—and yes, in Chelki, for the few combat vessels manned by the Omniarch's people had stayed outside the Vivarium to form a pitifully thin cordon around it, close in. He couldn't ask much of them except to stay where they were. He shot a look at Vez and listened for a moment to the orders Vez was snarling to the Hohdan ships. They were simple, and couldn't be anything else: charge for null, stand by for combat, and wait orders from *Luna*.

Luis Damiano's voice cut into the babble. "Commodore, do you have time to talk to the Omniarch?"

John hesitated a split second. "Yes—put him on!"

There was a bad substratum of static. He strained to make out the words. "John Braysen and Vez Do Han, we have seen the arrival of Vul fleets. We cannot ask you to fight an armada like this. Only a few minutes I ask—ten or fifteen, if you can provide as much. We have decided we must risk using the machinery I spoke of. If it works properly, the Vivarium will vanish from your sensors. Then, friends and allies, you may depart with our bottomless gratitude. If it does not—well, I cannot ask you to stay longer in any case. Fifteen minutes maximum. Do you agree?"

John looked at Vez. The Hohdan's face held an odd expression—perhaps Vez felt the way John did: determined to provide the fifteen minutes, unable to consider staying any longer than that, but unwilling even then to desert the gallant Chelki. Vez made the fist-open gesture.

John said tersely into the radio, "Fifteen minutes. Good luck."

Then he turned back to what few preparations he could make for a ludicrously feeble delaying action. But before he could transmit more than a couple of words, a smooth but violently amplified voice—a Vulmotean voice—blasted from the common-band receiver. "Vez Do Han?" it blared. "Please reply if you are anywhere in that laughable paltriness of ships."

Vez started, blinked, then grinned fiercely at John and made the fist-open gesture. John, as surprised as the Hohdan, understood Vez's meaning: if they want to parley, fine! Vez flicked a switch and leaned toward his pickup grille. "This is Vez Do Han. Who calls me, and why?"

Something between a chuckle and a purr came from the receiver grille. "My name is Bulvenorg. Until recently I was Second Senior Prime of the Vulmotean Defense Perimeter. Now I have been somewhat elevated, for a task the objectives of which you can doubtless guess. How do you like my little gathering, Hohdan? By the way, we met once, at a conference which made small alterations in the treaty between our two empires. I understand that you now occupy a position analagous to my recent one."

Vez, face haughtily calm, said, "I remember you well, Bulvenorg. Neither of us made much of a mark upon that conference. But we have a second chance here, eh? By the way, I too have a special mission at the moment. Oh—as to your gathering of ships—it is undeniably impressive, by former standards. I almost regret having to tell you that the values of battle have changed somewhat. I should *actually* regret having to prove that to you in a blunt way."

Again the purring chuckle. "You can avoid that necessity by the simplest of courses. And, while we are talking —was it you behind that little series of pin pricks against Bizh military bases? I know that the few miserable survivors of the human species, whose world was foolish enough to anger one of our less considerate vectors, staged those raids." A pause. "It occurs to me, Vez Do Han, that those renegades may be among you now. Would you do me the indulgence of confirming it? There is no real importance, of course."

John spoke before Vez could. It was foolish, but there was a hard anger in him now. "This is one of those renegades speaking. Is there something I can do for you, other than killing you?"

For a moment there was only the crackle of static. Even the babble from the other ships was hushed—and John realized that they were all listening to this exchange. Then the Vul's voice came again, serious and a little curious. "Are you by any chance John Braysen?"

John said flatly, "What of it?"

The Vul voice sighed. "Nothing much. It just confirms another guess of mine. . . . You have a splendid mind for military tactics, John Braysen. I regret that your species has been destroyed." A pause; then he spoke again to Vez Do Han. "A war between our empires, Hohdan, is no desire of yours or mine. Let us reach a civilized compromise. We will forget the small, though despicable, intrigue you perpetrated. I understand its purpose—and, if you care anymore, it has succeeded. Keep the few humans, if you feel sentimental attachment to them or if you consider them valuable mercenaries. Keep the few trivial ships of ours you somehow accumulated." A pause. "All I demand is yonder immensity at which we all keep glancing, and every last one of the Chelki, and that truly large ship which you are presumably aboard."

Vez glanced at John and grinned. Then he said into the pickup, "You ask of me booty that I do not own. All I know about that immensity you mention is that I saw a large number of Chelki aboard a miscellany of ships go into it. Since none have emerged again, I presume they mean to stay there. As you know, slaveholding is not one of Hohd's sins, so you can hardly ask me to help you retake escapees. As to this ship, aboard which I indeed am—"

The Vul voice interrupted sharply, "Consider, Vez Do Han—do you think my empire can afford to allow you exclusive access to Klee technology? Now, do not prattle nonsense any longer." To punctuate the demand, a heavy salvo of missiles suddenly appeared on mass detectors and radar screens—a mere gesture, considering what the Vul armada could launch. The interception lit up screens for an instant. Bulvenorg continued, "Should you decline to yield what I demand here, the result, I regret to inform you, will be an immediate all-out attack against your empire."

Vez flushed. "We are not Chelki, Bulvenorg, nor one small system, like Sol. There is nothing here that I am authorized to give away. As to your threats—"

Luis Damiano's voice, low but audible to John, came suddenly from the command circuit. "Commodore, the Omniarch just radioed. He says he's finished all preparations and that you are to null away right now!"

John's pulse leaped. Grinning, he gestured to Vez. Also, he glanced at the viewscreen showing the Vivarium and saw the few Chelki-crewed ships still outside—the armed ones—streaking for one end or the other to go inside. He poised his thumb above a computer-keyboard stud and said hurriedly into his command-circuit pickup: "All units—we're nulling in a few seconds, on computer lock-in!"

Vez, almost laughing aloud, stopped talking to the Vul and instead hurriedly repeated John's message in Hohdan to Vez's own ships. Then he made the fist-open gesture to John.

John squashed down hard on the "Null" stud.

And nothing happened.

Vez and John stared at each other, only half-hearing the Vul voice snarling from the receiver. Screens were already lighting up with flares as the first Vul salvos came into range and were intercepted. Already, John saw, the defense was almost saturated. He punched out a program, blurted into the pickup, "We're dodging on grav drive—local defense—" Dazed, he tried the "Null" stud again. It still didn't work, although all instruments said *Bertha* was charged and ready. Desperately, he punched the "Execute" stud for the grav-drive evasion.

Bertha didn't move.

The Vul voice had stopped now—but the Vul missiles hadn't. *Bertha* shuddered. A hit! But, though alarms were wailing and klaxons bleating, instruments said there was no penetration of the hull. The din was so loud now that John could hardly hear the voices shouting on the intercom. He turned it to maximum volume and leaned forward. ". . . don't we null?" Ralph Cole was nearly screaming.

John, stunned, looked at viewscreens, and an awful realization exploded over him.

All his other ships—and Vez Do Han's—were gone. *Bertha* was alone.

Another jar, as some Vul missile got through the desperate counterfire of small missiles, laser clusters, and rupters. Through his stunned bewilderment, John felt a sharp lance of pride at the way his men were fighting. But it was ridiculously futile. Even if the great hull didn't give way, the mere accumulation of heat would destroy the ship soon enough!

It was Vez who jabbed at a stud and shouted, "Damiano! *Get through to the Omniarch!*"

The Omniarch's voice, vastly amplified, came wearily above the din of hits, near-misses, and *Bertha's* own fighting noise. "On my honor, Vez Do Han—I am *not* holding you!" Some distracted Chelki talk in the background. "I am as astounded as you. John Braysen, are you listening? There are— Gods of space! All I can think of is that this Vivarium has automatic machinery programmed to defend itself—and that it includes holding close the Klee ship in our vicinity. We are scrambling over machinery—" The Omniarch suddenly stopped talking and took a deep breath. Then he resumed again. "Listen, friends, if you are locked to the Vivarium, that bond will be severed in less than two minutes. Unless we have calculated wrong, that is when we shall vanish."

John and Vez stared at each other in mutual numb astonishment. Then both looked suddenly toward the chronometer.

The jar of missile hits and detonations went on steadily. Someone, somewhere in the ship, bellowed with angry terror and was suddenly silent. Bart Lange blurted, "That's a hatch cover that went!"

John turned his head slowly to look at another bank of instruments. Which one represented that part of the ship?

His mind seemed to have gone on strike. Oh—that one. Yes, there was a holocaust in that particular bay. But the air conduits had automatically sealed off. He drew in an exhausted breath. What could anyone do now but watch that creeping chronometer needle. . . .

Then he contorted with such a knotted, inside-out sensation that he leaped from the chair, lost his footing, and sprawled on the deck.

Everyone in the control room was slowly picking himself off the deck. Bart Lange mumbled thickly, "What happened?"

John was still dazed from that weird twisting sensation —like a thousand nulls at the same instant—but he had wits enough to look at instruments and detectors. "We nulled, for one thing." He went awkwardly to his seat, squirmed into it, and leaned toward the intercom grille. "All hands, do whatever you can locally to secure ship and assess damage. We seem to be headed in toward the Hohdan Empire."

Luis Damaino's voice asked, "What in space happened, sir? I felt as if—"

John told him, "The Vivarium evidently kept us from nulling, or even moving on grav drive, until it leaped. That's what the Omniarch called it—'leaping.' Whether it nulled, or whether it went into the future, it vanished, and let us go. At least, that's what I guess—we'll have to play back sensor recordings." He paused, trying to think. "Oh —all the other ships nulled on schedule, I guess." He looked at Bart. "How many of the Armed Scouts are aboard?"

Bart blinked. "Four. At least, they were when—"

"Find out," John directed. He turned as a movement caught his eye. Lisa Duval had just come into the room. She was pale, but cool. He demanded, "Are you girls all right?"

She nodded slowly. "Just scared almost bald. What happened?"

He said, "We'll be a while finding out, I think. But we're out of trouble for now."

Bart Lange, standing before the from-null detector system, called, "John," and beckoned.

John went over beside him. Bart pointed to a familiar blue-violet blip nearer the center than the edge of the simulated sphere. "There it is. Or maybe that's just the same old marker, showing where they *were*." He chuckled and pointed to various tiny diffuse blobs. "The Vuls have broken into small groups—probably trying a new search pattern. I'll bet they're fit to bite each other!"

Vez, who'd walked over, said seriously, "So long as they stay out there, they aren't attacking Hohd. We'll be home long ahead of them. And we'll be ready, if they're foolish enough to carry through on the threat!"

Now that the excitement was over, John felt the *dron* thirst. He'd have to endure it—he couldn't afford to get drunk on even alcohol, now. He watched Lisa Duval leave to rejoin and reassure the women; then he went slowly back to his seat. He looked toward Vez. "Your ships will be home ahead of us. Is it all right with you if we go directly to that planet you gave us? If we may, we'll use that as a base while we look for something far away."

Vez said, "Of course. But I shall want one of your small ships, and a number of dispatch drones."

John automatically made the fist-open gesture. Then he looked wearily at the breakout timer.

Two hours and fifty-odd minutes to go.

The time crawled, as only null time can crawl. But even that slow creep was steady, and at long last the timepiece showed ten more minutes. Bart Lange was standing before the from-null detector system and frowning. "That knocking around we got must have jarred this out of adjustment. I can't even locate that planet's star."

John sighed. "Well, can you find that double binary? We can navigate from there."

"Yes, but even that doesn't look right. I think I remember that part of space. . . ."

Vez Do Han put in, "Instruments or not, we'll find it. I know the region like my backyard."

They did find the green planet, but it took them longer than they expected.

Breakout.

John took *Bertha* in slowly, until she was in atmosphere. He moved around to the night side, used radar to pinpoint the small lake and the meadow alongside it. He went lower, frowning. At least one of the four men there should be awake to answer a radio hail.

But no answer came. He went lower and used searchlights. Things didn't look right at all, and a very chill, very hard lump seemed to form in his stomach. He swallowed hard.

It wasn't until morning that they were sure. There was no Armed Scout around, though one had been left. There was a mass of metal where a few missiles had been stacked, but the place was completely overgrown with vines, and even a few trees towered above it. There was absolutely no sign that a shack had ever been there, nor any other hint of occupancy.

Slowly John looked up at Vez. "I think we'd better get to some civilized world as fast as we can. If there are any left."

Without looking puzzled, Vez slowly made the fist-open sign.

(24)

AFTER *Bertha* had orbited a peaceful-looking planet for
several hours—far out, to avoid frightening any more
inhabitants than necessary—Vez Do Han came back up in
the small grav boat he'd taken down and gave details of
what they already knew. "I could hardly talk to them," he
said, "the accent's changed so much. The written language,
I can still decipher—they have ancient writings, on non-
perishable metal, that have kept it from drifting much.
And I managed to piece together some of the legends."

John asked, "How long has it been? Do they know?"

"I tried to get some estimate; and I'd guess, eleven or
twelve thousand years. But I could be badly off. They
weren't really surprised to see me—I guess most of them
believe that their ancestors had an interstellar culture and
that some of it might still exist. I didn't even try to explain
that I was from their remote past—and that some of them
might even be descendants of mine." He managed a weak
grin. "I'm nowhere near as bad off as you thought you
were, John Braysen. The women down there look healthy
and friendly."

John stared at the deck for a minute. "Well, are you
going to join them? There are lots of gadgets aboard that
belong to you—not to mention the whole ship! Of course,
there may be other Hohdan worlds elsewhere, better
equipped to use them."

Vez sighed. "I think not. I'm not even sure I'd want to
dump space-age technology—and *Klee* technology—on a
people halfway between pastoral and early-machine ages.
I'll have to think about it for a while." He grinned at John.

"Will any of you mind if I and my four men stay with you for the time being?"

"Of course not! Most of us will settle on that planet you gave us a few thousand years ago, at least temporarily. But what about *Bertha?* She's yours, after all."

"I'm not sure about that either now, John Braysen. Let's call it a partnership, shall we? There are a few trips we ought to make."

"To see if the Vul Empire's still in business, you mean? Or other space cultures?"

"That's right."

John mused for a few minutes. Then he looked up. "There's another trip I'd like to make, eventually."

Vez smiled. "I imagine you mean to Earth."

Bertha didn't go anywhere from the green planet for nearly half a local year (slightly longer than Earth years), and then it was a journey of only two hundred hours, after which there was no doubt that the Vulmot Empire had gone the way of the Hohdan one. So, apparently, had the Bizh Empire—there were only a few small space cultures in either spiral arm, and those didn't seem militarily inclined.

There were signs—overgrown, in most cases, but signs —of a terrible interstellar war at least ten thousand years earlier that had blasted *all* space cultures, in this sector of the galaxy at least, back to near-savagery. But there was no way of learning details.

There were a few more, shorter, trips, during one of which Vez acquired a sweet, pleasant, lovely Hohdan bride (who called herself a "Freselian") and brought her home to the green planet. Finally, over a year and a half after the settlement on that world, John, with Bart Lange and Luis Damiano and Ralph Cole and some unmarried men —plus Lisa Duval—made the trip to Earth.

What with one thing and another, it wasn't for nearly another year that John saw Vez Do Han again.

Vez wanted to know what condition Earth was in.

"Well," John told him, "actually, we were dumbfounded

at first, though we've more or less figured it out now. Not that it was surprising to find practically all the radioactivity washed out of the air and soil by this time—but it seemed impossible that there should be plant life on the planet. But there it was—a blanket of mosslike growth all over nearly everything, green in some places, purplish or crimson in others. All the dead trees we'd seen before were gone, of course—fires must have finished them before long." He paused and stared at the simple bungalow where he lived now. (They were sitting a little way out on the meadow, sipping experimental local beer—a fairly successful experiment, at that.) "We'd been so sure all life was wiped out. But a few seeds, or spores, must have been alive, frozen into ice fields or deep underground where the bad stuff didn't reach them. And, after the stuff was mostly gone, a few found themselves in positions to sprout, and did." He drank more beer. "I still can't understand about the seas—maybe some life still survived, in the deeps where deadly compounds didn't get, or in ooze that didn't get stirred up too soon. In any case, Earth's seas are teeming with microscopic plant organisms that are putting oxygen back into the air at an amazing rate. As geological times go, I mean."

Vez asked, "What percentage now?"

"Over fourteen. It never fell below ten, apparently."

"Could you live there now?"

"We think so. But it wouldn't be worthwhile unless there were some way to boost the oxygen content a little more, fast. And we'll have to transplant some trees and grass and things from somewhere, and stock the continents with animals and the rivers and lakes with fish and whatnot."

"How about the seas? Are *they* too radioactive?"

"No, most of the stuff's settled out. Sea animals too, if we run across any that can adapt."

Vez sat smiling for a few minutes. "Well, have you any plans to start that sort of thing?"

"Oh, yes. In fact, we made a tour out along the spiral arm, looking for suitable species. We think we've found some. For that matter, some of the trees right here on this planet, and a few animal species, might adapt all right. Next trip, we'll be trying a few."

Vez sighed. "Did you visit any of the smaller empires out along the arm? I mean, the places where ships used to stop, trade crossroads, the spectacular worlds. . . ."

"We looked in on some. A lot of formerly populated worlds are dead now. That war . . ." He paused. "We even dropped in on Drongail, out of curiosity. It's just a dirty rock now. Not even a sprig of *dron* growing anywhere."

Vez grinned. "How did that affect you?"

John leaned over in his chair and put his arm around Lisa's shoulders. "I didn't feel the faintest twinge. Honestly."